RESERVED
£3.50

# THE TERROR

## A FANTASY

BY

ARTHUR MACHEN

AUTHOR OF
"THE BOWMEN"

LONDON
DUCKWORTH & CO.
3 HENRIETTA STREET, COVENT GARDEN, W.C.

*First published* 1917

PRINTED IN GREAT BRITAIN BY THE COMPLETE PRESS,
WEST NORWOOD, ENGLAND

# CHAPTER I

AFTER two years we are turning once more to the morning's news with a sense of appetite and glad expectation. There were thrills at the beginning of the war; the thrill of horror and of a doom that seemed at once incredible and certain; this was when Namur fell and the German host swelled like a flood over the French fields, and drew very near to the walls of Paris. Then we felt the thrill of exultation when the good news came that the awful tide had been turned back, that Paris and the world were safe; for awhile at all events.

Then for days we hoped for more news as good as this or better. Has Von Kluck been surrounded? Not to-day, but perhaps he will be surrounded to-morrow. But the days became weeks, the weeks drew out to months; the battle in the West seemed frozen. Now and again things were done that seemed hopeful, with promise of events still better. But Neuve Chapelle and Loos dwindled into disappointments as their tale was told fully; the lines in the West remained, for all practical purposes of victory, immobile. Nothing seemed to happen, there was nothing to read save the record of operations that were clearly trifling and insignificant. People speculated as to the reason of this inaction; the hopeful said that Joffre had a plan, that he was "nibbling," others declared that we were short of munitions, others again that the new levies were not yet ripe for battle. So the months went by, and almost two years of war had been completed before the motionless English line began to stir and quiver as if it awoke from a long sleep, and began to roll onward, overwhelming the enemy.

    .      .      .      .

The secret of the long inaction of the British Armies has been well kept. On the one hand it was rigorously protected by the censorship, which severe, and sometimes severe to the point of absurdity—" the captains and the . . . depart," for instance— became in this particular matter ferocious. As soon as the real significance of that which was happening, or beginning to happen, was perceived by the authorities, an underlined circular was issued to the newspaper proprietors of Great Britain and Ireland. It warned each proprietor that he might impart the contents of this circular to one other person only, such person being the responsible editor of his paper, who was to keep the communication secret under the severest penalties. The circular forbade any mention of certain events that had taken place, that might take place ; it forbade any kind of allusion to these events or any hint of their existence, or of the possibility of their existence, not only in the Press, but in any form whatever. The subject was not to be alluded to in conversation, it was not to be hinted at, however obscurely, in letters ; the very existence of the circular, its subject apart, was to be a dead secret.

These measures were successful. A wealthy newspaper proprietor of the North, warmed a little at the end of the Throwsters' Feast (which was held as usual, it will be remembered), ventured to say to the man next to him : " How awful it would be, wouldn't it, if . . ." His words were repeated, as proof, one regrets to say, that it was time for " old Arnold " to " pull himself together " ; and he was fined a thousand pounds. Then, there was the case of an obscure weekly paper published in the

county town of an agricultural district in
Wales. The *Meiros Observer* (we will call it)
was issued from a stationer's back premises,
and filled its four pages with accounts of
local flower shows, fancy fairs at vicarages,
reports of parish councils, and rare bathing
fatalities. It also issued a visitors' list,
which has been known to contain six
names.

This enlightened organ printed a paragraph, which nobody noticed, which was
very like paragraphs that small country
newspapers have long been in the habit of
printing, which could hardly give so much
as a hint to anyone—to anyone, that is, who
was not fully instructed in the secret. As
a matter of fact, this piece of intelligence
got into the paper because the proprietor,
who was also the editor, incautiously left
the last processes of this particular issue to
the staff, who was the Lord-High-Every-
thing-Else of the establishment ; and the
staff put in a bit of gossip he had heard in
the market to fill up two inches on the back
page. But the result was that the *Meiros
Observer* ceased to appear, owing to " unto-
ward circumstances " as the proprietor said ;
and he would say no more. No more, that
is, by way of explanation, but a great deal

more by way of execration of " damned,
prying busybodies."

    .     .     .

Now a censorship that is sufficiently
minute and utterly remorseless can do
amazing things in the way of hiding . . .
what it wants to hide. Before the war,
one would have thought otherwise ; one
would have said that, censor or no censor,
the fact of the murder at X or the fact of
the bank robbery at Y would certainly become known ; if not through the Press, at
all events through rumour and the passage
of the news from mouth to mouth. And this
would be true—of England three hundred
years ago, and of savage tribelands of to-
day. But we have grown of late to such
a reverence for the printed word and
such a reliance on it, that the old
faculty of disseminating news by word
of mouth has become atrophied. Forbid
the Press to mention the fact that Jones
has been murdered, and it is marvellous
how few people will hear of it, and of
those who hear how few will credit the
story that they have heard. You meet
a man in the train who remarks that
he has been told something about a murder

in Southwark ; there is all the difference
in the world between the impression you
receive from such a chance communication
and that given by half a dozen lines of
print with name, and street and date
and all the facts of the case. People
in trains repeat all sorts of tales, many of
them false ; newspapers do not print
accounts of murders that have not been
committed.

Then another consideration that has
made for secrecy. I may have seemed to
say that the old office of rumour no longer
exists ; I shall be reminded of the strange
legend of " the Russians " and the mytho-
logy of the " Angels of Mons." But let me
point out, in the first place, that both these
absurdities depended on the papers for
their wide dissemination. If there had
been no newspapers or magazines Russians
and Angels would have made but a brief,
vague appearance of the most shadowy
kind—a few would have heard of them,
fewer still would have believed in them,
they would have been gossiped about
for a bare week or two, and so they would
have vanished away.

And, then, again, the very fact of these
vain rumours and fantastic tales having

been so widely believed for a time was fatal to the credit of any stray mutterings that may have got abroad. People had been taken in twice ; they had seen how grave persons, men of credit, had preached and lectured about the shining forms that had saved the British Army at Mons, or had testified to the trains, packed with grey-coated Muscovites, rushing through the land at dead of night : and now there was a hint of something more amazing than either of the discredited legends. But this time there was no word of confirmation to be found in daily paper, or weekly review, or parish magazine, and so the few that heard either laughed, or, being serious, went home and jotted down notes for essays on " War-time Psychology : Collective Delusions."

I followed neither of these courses. For before the secret circular had been issued my curiosity had somehow been aroused by certain paragraphs concerning a " Fatal Accident to Well-known Airman." The pro-peller of the airplane had been shattered, apparently by a collision with a flight of pigeons ; the blades had been broken and the machine had fallen like lead to the

earth. And soon after I had seen this
account, I heard of some very odd circumstances relating to an explosion in a
great munition factory in the Midlands.
I thought I saw the possibility of a connexion between two very different events.


It has been pointed out to me by friends
who have been good enough to read this
record, that certain phrases I have used may
give the impression that I ascribe all the
delays of the war on the Western front
to the extraordinary circumstances which
occasioned the issue of the Secret Circular.
Of course this is not the case, there were
many reasons for the immobility of our lines
from October 1914 to July 1916. These
causes have been evident enough and have
been openly discussed and deplored. But
behind them was something of infinitely
greater moment. We lacked men, but men
were pouring into the new army ; we were
short of shells, but when the shortage was
proclaimed the nation set itself to mend
this matter with all its energy. We could
undertake to supply the defects of our army
both in men and munitions—*if* the new
and incredible danger could be overcome.

It has been overcome ; rather, perhaps, it has ceased to exist ; and the secret may now be told.

I have said my attention was attracted by an account of the death of a well-known airman. I have not the habit of preserving cuttings, I am sorry to say, so that I cannot be precise as to the date of this event. To the best of my belief it was either towards the end of May or the beginning of June 1915. The newspaper paragraph announcing the death of Flight-Lieutenant Western-Reynolds was brief enough ; accidents, and fatal accidents, to the men who are storming the air for us are, unfortunately, by no means so rare as to demand an elaborated notice. But the manner in which Western-Reynolds met his death struck me as extraordinary, inasmuch as it revealed a new danger in the element that we have lately conquered. He was brought down, as I said, by a flight of birds ; of pigeons, as appeared by what was found on the bloodstained and shattered blades of the propeller. An eye-witness of the accident, a fellow-officer, described how Western-Reynolds set out from the aero-drome on a fine afternoon, there being hardly any wind. He was going to France ;

he had made the journey to and fro half a dozen times or more, and felt perfectly secure and at ease.

"'Wester' rose to a great height at once, and we could scarcely see the machine. I was turning to go when one of the fellows called out, 'I say! What's this?' He pointed up, and we saw what looked like a black cloud coming from the south at a tremendous rate. I saw at once it wasn't a cloud; it came with a swirl and a rush quite different from any cloud I've ever seen. But for a second I couldn't make out exactly what it was. It altered its shape and turned into a great crescent, and wheeled and veered about as if it was looking for something. The man who had called out had got his glasses, and was staring for all he was worth. Then he shouted that it was a tremendous flight of birds, 'thousands of them.' They went on wheeling and beating about high up in the air, and we were watching them, thinking it was interesting, but not supposing that they would make any difference to 'Wester,' who was just about out of sight. His machine was just a speck. Then the two arms of the crescent drew in as quick as lightning, and these thousands of birds shot in a solid mass right up there across the sky, and flew away somewhere about nor'-nor'-by-west. Then Henley, the man with the glasses, called out, ' He's down ! ' and started running, and I went after him. We got a car and as we were going along Henley told me that he'd seen the machine drop dead, as if it came out of that cloud of birds. He thought then that they must have mucked up the propeller somehow. That turned out to be the case. We found the propeller blades all broken and covered with blood and pigeon feathers, and carcases of the birds had got wedged in between the blades, and were sticking to them."

This was the story that the young airman told one evening in a small company. He did not speak " in confidence," so I have no hesitation in reproducing what he said. Naturally, I did not take a verbatim note of his conversation, but I have something of a knack of remembering talk that interests me, and I think my reproduction is very near to the tale that I heard. And let it be noted that the flying man told his story without any sense or indication of a sense that the incredible, or all but the incredible, had happened. So far as he knew, he said,

it was the first accident of the kind. Airmen in France had been bothered once or
twice by birds—he thought they were eagles
—flying viciously at them, but poor old
" Wester " had been the first man to come
up against a flight of some thousands of
pigeons.

"And perhaps I shall be the next," he
added, " but why look for trouble ? Anyhow, I'm going to see *Toodle-oo* to-morrow
afternoon."

.     .     .     .

Well, I heard the story, as one hears all
the varied marvels and terrors of the air ; as
one heard some years ago of " air pockets,"
strange gulfs or voids in the atmosphere
into which airmen fell with great peril ; or
as one heard of the experience of the airman
who flew over the Cumberland mountains
in the burning summer of 1911, and as he
swam far above the heights was suddenly
and vehemently blown upwards, the hot
air from the rocks striking his plane as if
it has been a blast from a furnace chimney.
We have just begun to navigate a strange
region ; we must expect to encounter
strange adventures, strange perils. And
here a new chapter in the chronicles of these

perils and adventures had been opened by the death of Western-Reynolds ; and no doubt invention and contrivance would presently hit on some way of countering the new danger.

It was, I think, about a week or ten days after the airman's death that my business called me to a northern town, the name of which, perhaps, had better remain unknown. My mission was to inquire into certain charges of extravagance which had been laid against the working people, that is, the munition workers of this especial town. It was said that the men who used to earn £2 10s. a week were now getting from seven to eight pounds, that " bits of girls " were being paid two pounds instead of seven or eight shillings, and that, in consequence, there was an orgie of foolish extravagance. The girls, I was told, were eating chocolates at four, five, and six shillings a pound, the women were ordering thirty-pound pianos which they couldn't play, and the men bought gold chains at ten and twenty guineas apiece.

I dived into the town in question and found, as usual, that there was a mixture of truth and exaggeration in the stories that I had heard. Gramophones, for example :

they cannot be called in strictness neces-
saries, but they were undoubtedly finding a
ready sale, even in the more expensive
brands.   And I thought that there were a
great many very spick and span perambulators to be seen on the pavement ; smart
perambulators, painted in tender shades of
colour and expensively fitted.

" And how can you be surprised if people
will have a bit of a fling ? " a worker said to
me.   " We're seeing money for the first
time in our lives, and it's bright.   And we
work hard for it, and we risk our lives
to get it.   You've heard of explosion
yonder ? "

He mentioned certain works on the outskirts of the town.   Of course, neither the
name of the works nor of the town had been
printed ;   there had been a brief notice of
" Explosion at Munition Works in the
Northern District : Many Fatalities."   The
working man told me about it, and added
some dreadful details.

" They wouldn't let their folks see bodies ;
screwed them up in coffins as they found
them in shop.   The gas had done it."

" Turned their faces black, you mean ? "

" Nay.   They were all as if they had
been bitten to pieces."

This was a strange gas.

I asked the man in the northern town all sorts of questions about the extraordinary explosion of which he had spoken to me. But he had very little more to say. As I have noted already, secrets that may not be printed are often deeply kept ; last summer there were very few people outside high official circles who knew anything about the " Tanks," of which we have all been talking lately, though these strange instruments of war were being exercised and tested in a park not far from London. So the man who told me of the explosion in the munition factory was most likely genuine in his profession that he knew nothing more of the disaster. I found out that he was a smelter employed at a furnace on the other side of the town to the ruined factory ; he didn't know even what they had been making there ; some very dangerous high explosive, he supposed. His information was really nothing more than a bit of gruesome gossip, which he had heard probably at third or fourth or fifth hand. The horrible detail of faces " as if they had been bitten to pieces " had made its violent impression on him, that was all.

I gave him up and took a tram to the

district of the disaster ; a sort of industrial
suburb, five miles from the centre of the
town. When I asked for the factory, I was
told that it was no good my going to it as
there was nobody there. But I found it ;
a raw and hideous shed with a walled yard
about it, and a shut gate. I looked for signs
of destruction, but there was nothing. The
roof was quite undamaged ; and again it
struck me that this had been a strange
accident. There had been an explosion of
sufficient violence to kill workpeople in the
building, but the building itself showed no
wounds or scars.

A man came out of the gate and locked
it behind him. I began to ask him some
sort of question, or rather, I began to
" open " for a question with " A terrible
business here, they tell me," or some such
phrase of convention. I got no farther.
The man asked me if I saw a policeman
walking down the street. I said I did, and
I was given the choice of getting about my
business forthwith or of being instantly
given in charge as a spy. " Th'ast better
be gone and quick about it," was, I think,
his final advice, and I took it.

Well, I had come literally up against a
brick wall. Thinking the problem over,

I could only suppose that the smelter or his informant had twisted the phrases of the story. The smelter had said the dead men's faces were " bitten to pieces " ; this might be an unconscious perversion of " eaten away." That phrase might describe well enough the effect of strong acids, and, for all I knew of the processes of munition-making, such acids might be used and might explode with horrible results in some perilous stage of their admixture.

It was a day or two later that the accident to the airman, Western-Reynolds, came into my mind. For one of those instants which are far shorter than any measure of time there flashed out the possibility of a link between the two disasters. But here was a wild impossibility, and I drove it away. And yet I think that the thought, mad as it seemed, never left me ; it was the secret light that at last guided me through a sombre grove of enigmas.

It was about this time, so far as the date can be fixed, that a whole district, one might say a whole county, was visited by a series of extraordinary and terrible calamities, which were the more terrible inasmuch as they continued for some time to be inscrutable mysteries. It is, indeed, doubtful whether these awful events do not still remain mysteries to many of those concerned ; for before the inhabitants of this part of the country had time to join one link of evidence to another the circular was issued, and thenceforth no one knew how to distinguish undoubted fact from wild and extravagant surmise.

The district in question is in the far west of Wales ; I shall call it, for convenience, Meirion. In it there is one seaside town of some repute with holiday-makers for five or six weeks in the summer, and dotted about the county there are three or four small old towns that seem drooping in a slow decay, sleepy and grey with age and forgetfulness. They remind me of what I have read of towns in the west of Ireland. Grass grows between the uneven stones of the pavements, the signs above the shop windows decline, half the letters of these signs are missing, here and there a house has been pulled down, or has been allowed to slide into ruin, and wild greenery springs up through the fallen stones, and there is silence in all the streets. And, it is to be noted, these are not places that were once magnificent. The Celts have never had the art of building, and so far as I can see, such towns as Towy and Merthyr Tegveth and Meiros must have been always much as they are now, clusters of poorish, meanly-built houses, ill-kept and down at heel.

And these few towns are thinly scattered over a wild country where north is divided from south by a wilder mountain range. One of these places is sixteen miles from any station; the others are doubtfully and deviously connected by single-line railways served by rare trains that pause and stagger and hesitate on their slow journey up mountain passes, or stop for half an hour or more at lonely sheds called stations, situated in the midst of desolate marshes. A few years ago I travelled with an Irishman on one of these queer lines, and he looked to right and saw the bog with its yellow and blue grasses and stagnant pools, and he looked to left and saw a ragged hill-side, set with grey stone walls. "I can hardly believe," he said, "that I'm not still in the wilds of Ireland."

Here, then, one sees a wild and divided and scattered region, a land of outland hills and secret and hidden valleys. I know white farms on this coast which must be separated by two hours of hard, rough

walking from any other habitation, which
are invisible from any other house. And
inland, again, the farms are often ringed
about by thick groves of ash, planted by
men of old days to shelter their roof-trees
from rude winds of the mountain and
stormy winds of the sea ; so that these
places, too, are hidden away, to be surmised
only by the wood smoke that rises from the
green surrounding leaves. A Londoner
must see them to believe in them ; and even
then he can scarcely credit their utter
isolation.

Such, then in the main is Meirion, and
on this land in the early summer of last
year terror descended—a terror without
shape, such as no man there had ever
known.

It began with the tale of a little child
who wandered out into the lanes to pick
flowers one sunny afternoon, and never came
back to the cottage on the hill.

# CHAPTER II

THE child who was lost came from a lonely cottage that stands on the slope of a steep hillside called the Allt, or the height. The land about it is wild and ragged ; here the growth of gorse and bracken, here a marshy hollow of reeds and rushes, marking the course of the stream from some hidden well, here thickets of dense and tangled under-growth, the outposts of the wood. Down through this broken and uneven ground a path leads to the lane at the bottom of the valley ; then the land rises again and swells up to the cliffs over the sea, about a quarter of a mile away. The little girl, Gertrude Morgan, asked her mother if she might go down to the lane and pick the purple flowers—these were orchids—that grew there, and her mother gave her leave, telling her she must be sure to be back by tea-time, as there was apple-tart for tea.

She never came back. It was supposed that she must have crossed the road and gone to the cliff's edge, possibly in order to pick the sea-pinks that were then in full blossom. She must have slipped, they said, and fallen into the sea, two hundred feet below. And, it may be said at once, that

there was no doubt some truth in this conjecture, though it stopped very far short
of the whole truth. The child's body must
have been carried out by the tide, for it
was never found.

The conjecture of a false step or of a fatal
slide on the slippery turf that slopes down
to the rocks was accepted as being the only
explanation possible. People thought the
accident a strange one because, as a rule,
country children living by the cliffs and the
sea become wary at an early age, and
Gertrude Morgan was almost ten years old.
Still, as the neighbours said, " that's how it
must have happened, and it's a great pity,
to be sure." But this would not do when
in a week's time a strong young labourer
failed to come to his cottage after the day's
work. His body was found on the rocks six
or seven miles from the cliffs where the
child was supposed to have fallen ; he was
going home by a path that he had used
every night of his life for eight or nine
years, that he used of dark nights in perfect
security, knowing every inch of it. The
police asked if he drank, but he was a
teetotaller ; if he were subject to fits, but
he wasn't. And he was not murdered for
his wealth, since agricultural labourers are

not wealthy. It was only possible again to talk of slippery turf and a false step ; but people began to be frightened. Then a woman was found with her neck broken at the bottom of a disused quarry near Llanfihangel, in the middle of the county. The " false step " theory was eliminated here, for the quarry was guarded with a natural hedge of gorse bushes. One would have to struggle and fight through sharp thorns to destruction in such a place as this ; and indeed the gorse bushes were broken as if some one had rushed furiously through them, just above the place where the woman's body was found. And this was strange : there was a dead sheep lying beside her in the pit, as if the woman and the sheep together had been chased over the brim of the quarry. But chased by whom, or by what ? And then there was a new form of terror.

This was in the region of the marshes under the mountain. A man and his son, a lad of fourteen or fifteen, set out early one morning to work and never reached the farm where they were bound. Their way skirted the marsh, but it was broad, firm and well metalled, and it had been raised about two feet above the bog. But when

search was made in the evening of the same
day Phillips and his son were found dead
in the marsh, covered with black slime and
pond-weed. And they lay some ten yards
from the path, which, it would seem, they
must have left deliberately. It was useless,
of course, to look for tracks in the black
ooze, for if one threw a big stone into it a
few seconds removed all marks of the dis-
turbance. The men who found the two
bodies beat about the verges and purlieus
of the marsh in hope of finding some trace
of the murderers ; they went to and fro over
the rising ground where the black cattle
were grazing, they searched the alder
thickets by the brook ; but they discovered
nothing.

Most horrible of all these horrors, perhaps,
was the affair of the Highway, a lonely
and unfrequented by-road that winds for
many miles on high and lonely land.
Here, a mile from any other dwelling, stands
a cottage on the edge of a dark wood. It
was inhabited by a labourer named Williams, his wife, and their three children.
One hot summer's evening, a man who had
been doing a day's gardening at a rectory
three or four miles away, passed the cottage,
and stopped for a few minutes to chat

with Williams, the labourer, who was pottering about his garden, while the children were playing on the path by the door. The two talked of their neighbours and of the potatoes till Mrs. Williams appeared at the doorway and said supper was ready, and Williams turned to go into the house. This was about eight o'clock, and in the ordinary course the family would have their supper and be in bed by nine, or by half-past nine at latest. At ten o'clock that night the local doctor was driving home along the Highway. His horse shied violently and then stopped dead just opposite the gate to the cottage. The doctor got down, frightened at what he saw; and there on the roadway lay Williams, his wife, and the three children, stone dead, all of them. Their skulls were battered in as if by some heavy iron instrument; their faces were beaten into a pulp.

# CHAPTER III

I⊤ is [not easy to make any picture of the horror that lay dark on the hearts of the people of Meirion. It was no longer possible to believe or to pretend to believe that these men and women and children had met their deaths through strange accidents. The little girl and the young labourer might have slipped and fallen over the cliffs, but the woman who lay dead with the dead sheep at the bottom of the quarry, the two men who had been lured into the ooze of the marsh, the family who were found murdered on the Highway before their own cottage door ; in these cases there could be no room for the supposition of accident. It seemed as if it were impossible to frame any conjecture or outline of a conjecture that would account for these hideous and, as it seemed, utterly purposeless crimes. For a time people said that there must be a madman at large, a sort of country variant of Jack the Ripper, some horrible pervert who was possessed by the passion of death, who prowled darkling about that lonely land, hiding in woods and in wild places, always watching and seeking for the victims of his desire.

Indeed, Dr. Lewis, who found poor Williams, his wife and children miserably slaughtered on the Highway, was convinced at first that the presence of a concealed madman in the countryside offered the only possible solution to the difficulty.

" I felt sure," he said to me afterwards, " that the Williams's had been killed by a homicidal maniac. It was the nature of the poor creatures' injuries that convinced me that this was the case. Some years ago —thirty-seven or thirty-eight years ago as a matter of fact—I had something to do with a case which on the face of it had a strong likeness to the Highway murder. At that time I had a practice at Usk, in Monmouthshire. A whole family living in a cottage by the roadside were murdered one evening ; it was called, I think, the Llangibby murder ; the cottage was near the village of that name. The murderer was caught in Newport ; he was a Spanish sailor, named Garcia, and it appeared that he had killed father, mother, and the three children for the sake of the brass works of an old Dutch clock, which were found on him when he was arrested.

" Garcia had been serving a month's imprisonment in Usk Gaol for some small theft, and on his release he set out to walk to Newport, nine or ten miles away ; no doubt to get another ship. He passed the cottage and saw the man working in his garden. Garcia stabbed him with his sailor's knife. The wife rushed out ; he stabbed her. Then he went into the cottage and stabbed the three children, tried to set the place on fire, and made off with the clockworks. That looked like the deed of a madman, but Garcia wasn't mad—they hanged him, I may say—he was merely a man of a very low type, a degenerate who hadn't the slightest value for human life. I am not sure, but I think he came from one of the Spanish islands, where the people are said to be degenerates, very likely from too much inter-breeding.

" But my point is that Garcia stabbed to kill and did kill, with one blow in each case. There was no senseless hacking and slashing. Now those poor people on the Highway had their heads smashed to pieces by what must have been a storm of blows. Any one of them would have been fatal, but the murderer must have gone on raining blows with his iron hammer on people who were already stone dead. And *that* sort of thing is the work of a madman, and nothing but a madman. That's how I argued the matter out to myself just after the event.

" I was utterly wrong, monstrously wrong. But who could have suspected the truth ? "

Thus Dr. Lewis, and I quote him, or the substance of him, as representative of most of the educated opinion of the district at the beginnings of the terror. People seized on this theory largely because it offered at least the comfort of an explanation, and any explanation, even the poorest, is better than an intolerable and terrible mystery. Besides, Dr. Lewis's theory was plausible ; it explained the lack of purpose that seemed to characterize the murders. And yet— there were difficulties even from the first. It was hardly possible that a strange madman should be able to keep hidden in a countryside where any stranger is instantly noted and noticed ; sooner or later he would be seen as he prowled along the lanes or across the wild places. Indeed, a drunken, cheerful, and altogether harmless tramp was arrested by a farmer and his man in the fact and act of sleeping off beer under a hedge ; but the vagrant was able to prove complete and undoubted alibis, and was soon allowed to go on his wandering way.

c

Then another theory, or rather a variant of Dr. Lewis's theory, was started. This was to the effect that the person responsible for the outrages was, indeed, a madman ; but a madman only at intervals. It was one of the members of the Porth Club, a certain Mr. Remnant, who was supposed to have originated this more subtle explanation. Mr. Remnant was a middle-aged man, who, having nothing particular to do, read a great many books by way of conquering the hours. He talked to the club —doctors, retired colonels, parsons, lawyers —about " personality," quoted various psychological text-books in support of his contention that personality was sometimes fluid and unstable, went back to " Dr. Jekyll and Mr. Hyde " as good evidence of this proposition, and laid stress on Dr. Jekyll's speculation that the human soul, so far from being one and indivisible, might possibly turn out to be a mere polity, a state in which dwelt many strange and incongruous citizens, whose characters were not merely unknown but altogether unsurmised by that form of consciousness which so rashly assumed that it was not only the president of the republic but also its sole citizen.

" The long and the short of it is," Mr. Remnant concluded, " that any one of us may be the murderer, though he hasn't the faintest notion of the fact.  Take Llewelyn there."

Mr. Payne Llewelyn was an elderly lawyer, a rural Tulkinghorn.  He was the hereditary solicitor to the Morgans of Pentwyn.  This does not sound anything tremendous to the Saxons of London ; but the style is far more than noble to the Celts of West Wales ; it is immemorial ; Teilo Sant was of the collaterals of the first known chief of the race.  And Mr. Payne Llewelyn did his best to look like the legal adviser of this ancient house.  He was weighty, he was cautious, he was sound, he was secure. I have compared him to Mr. Tulkinghorn of Lincoln's Inn Fields ; but Mr. Llewelyn would most certainly never have dreamed of employing his leisure in peering into the cupboards where the family skeletons were hidden.  Supposing such cupboards to have existed, Mr. Payne Llewelyn would have risked large out-of-pocket expenses to furnish them with double, triple, impregnable locks.  He was a new man, an *advena*, certainly ;  for he was partly of the Conquest, being descended on one side from Sir

Payne Turberville ; but he meant to stand by the old stock.

" Take Llewelyn now," said Mr. Remnant. " Look here, Llewelyn, can you produce evidence to show where you were on the night those people were murdered on the Highway ?   I thought not."

Mr. Llewelyn, an elderly man, as I have said, hesitated before speaking.

" I thought not," Remnant went on. " Now I say that it is perfectly possible that Llewelyn may be dealing death throughout Meirion, although in his present personality he may not have the faintest suspicion that there is another Llewelyn within him, a Llewelyn who follows murder as a fine art."

Mr. Payne Llewelyn did not at all relish Mr. Remnant's suggestion that he might well be a secret murderer, ravening for blood, remorseless as a wild beast. He thought the phrase about his following murder as a fine art was both nonsensical and in the worst taste, and his opinion was not changed when Remnant pointed out that it was used by De Quincey in the title of one of his most famous essays.

" If you had allowed me to speak," he

said with some coldness of manner, " I would have told you that on Tuesday last, the night on which those unfortunate people were murdered on the Highway I was staying at the Angel Hotel, Cardiff. I had business in Cardiff, and I was detained till Wednesday afternoon."

Having given this satisfactory alibi, Mr. Payne Llewelyn left the club, and did not go near it for the rest of the week.

Remnant explained to those who stayed in the smoking-room that, of course, he had merely used Mr. Llewelyn as a concrete example of his theory, which, he persisted, had the support of a considerable body of evidence.

" There are several cases of double personality on record," he declared. " And I say again that it is quite possible that these murders may have been committed by one of us in his secondary personality. Why, I may be the murderer in my Remnant B. state, though Remnant A. knows nothing whatever about it, and is perfectly convinced that he could not kill a fowl, much less a whole family. Isn't it so, Lewis ? "

Dr. Lewis said it was so, in theory, but he thought not in fact.

" Most of the cases of double or multiple

personality that have been investigated,"
he said, " have been in connexion with the
very dubious experiments of hypnotism, or
the still more dubious experiments of
spiritualism. All that sort of thing, in my
opinion, is like tinkering with the works of
a clock—amateur tinkering, I mean. You
fumble about with the wheels and cogs and
bits of mechanism that you don't really
know anything about ; and then you find
your clock going backwards or striking 240
at tea-time. And I believe it's just the
same thing with these psychical research
experiments ; the secondary personality is
very likely the result of the tinkering and
fumbling with a very delicate apparatus
that we know nothing about. Mind, I can't
say that it's impossible for one of us to
be the Highway murderer in his B. state,
as Remnant puts it. But I think it's extremely improbable. Probability is the
guide of life, you know, Remnant," said
Dr. Lewis, smiling at that gentleman, as if to
say that he also had done a little reading
in his day. " And it follows, therefore, that
improbability is also the guide of life.
When you get a very high degree of probability, that is, you are justified in taking
it as a certainty ; and on the other hand, if a

supposition is highly improbable, you are justified in treating it as an impossible one. That is, in nine hundred and ninety-nine cases out of a thousand."

" How about the thousandth case ? " said Remnant. " Supposing these extraordinary crimes constitute the thousandth case ? "

The doctor smiled and shrugged his shoulders, being tired of the subject. But for some little time highly respectable members of Porth society would look suspiciously at one another wondering whether, after all, there mightn't be " something in it." However, both Mr. Remnant's somewhat crazy theory and Dr. Lewis's plausible theory became untenable when two more victims of an awful and mysterious death were offered up in sacrifice, for a man was found dead in the Llanfihangel quarry, where the woman had been discovered. And on the same day a girl of fifteen was found broken on the jagged rocks under the cliffs near Porth. Now, it appeared that these two deaths must have occurred at about the same time, within an hour of one another, certainly ; and the distance between the quarry and the cliffs by Black Rock is certainly twenty miles.

" A motor could do it," one man said.

But it was pointed out that there was no high road between the two places ; indeed, it might be said that there was no road at all between them. There was a network of deep, narrow, and tortuous lanes that wandered into one another at all manner of queer angles for, say, seventeen miles ; this in the middle, as it were, between Black Rock and the quarry at Llanfihangel. But to get to the high land of the cliffs one had to take a path that went through two miles of fields ; and the quarry lay a mile away from the nearest by-road in the midst of gorse and bracken and broken land. And, finally, there was no track of motor-car or motor-bicycle in the lanes which must have been followed to pass from one place to the other.

" What about an airplane, then ? " said the man of the motor-car theory. Well, there was certainly an aerodrome not far from one of the two places of death ; but somehow, nobody believed that the Flying Corps harboured a homicidal maniac. It seemed clear, therefore, that there must be more than one person concerned in the terror of Meirion. And Dr. Lewis himself abandoned his own theory.

" As I said to Remnant at the Club," he remarked, " improbability is the guide of life. I can't believe that there are a pack of madmen or even two madmen at large in the country. I give it up."

And now a fresh circumstance or set of circumstances became manifest to confound judgment and to awaken new and wild surmises. For at about this time people realized that none of the dreadful events that were happening all about them was so much as mentioned in the Press. I have already spoken of the fate of the *Meiros Observer*. This paper was suppressed by the authorities because it had inserted a brief paragraph about some person who had been " found dead under mysterious circumstances " ; I think that paragraph referred to the first death of Llanfihangel quarry. Thenceforth, horror followed on horror, but no word was printed in any of the local journals. The curious went to the newspaper offices—there were two left in the county—but found nothing save a firm refusal to discuss the matter. And the Cardiff papers were drawn and found blank ; and the London Press was apparently ignorant of the fact that crimes that had no parallel were terrorizing a whole country-

side. Everybody wondered what could
have happened, what was happening ; and
then it was whispered that the coroner
would allow no inquiry to be made as to
these deaths of darkness.

" In consequence of instructions received
from the Home Office," one coroner was
understood to have said, " I have to tell the
jury that their business will be to hear the
medical evidence and to bring in a verdict
immediately in accordance with that evidence. I shall disallow all questions."

One jury protested. The foreman refused
to bring in any verdict at all.

" Very good," said the coroner. " Then
I beg to inform you, Mr. Foreman and
gentlemen of the jury, that under the
Defence of the Realm Act I have power to
supersede your functions, and to enter a
verdict according to the evidence which has
been laid before the Court as if it had been
the verdict of you all."

The foreman and jury collapsed and
accepted what they could not avoid. But
the rumours that got abroad of all this,
added to the known fact that the terror was
ignored in the Press, no doubt by official
command, increased the panic that was now
arising, and gave it a new direction. Clearly,

people reasoned, these Government restrictions and prohibitions could only refer to the war, to some great danger in connexion with the war. And that being so, it followed that the outrages which must be kept so secret were the work of the enemy, that is of concealed German agents.

## CHAPTER IV

Iт is time, I think, for me to make one point clear. I began this history with certain references to an extraordinary accident to an airman whose machine fell to the ground after collision with a huge flock of pigeons ; and then to an explosion in a northern munition factory, an explosion, as I noted, of a very singular kind. Then I deserted the neighbourhood of London, and the northern district, and dwelt on a mysterious and terrible series of events which occurred in the summer of 1915 in a Welsh county, which I have named, for convenience, Meirion.

Well, let it be understood at once that all this detail that I have given about the occurrences in Meirion does not imply that the county in the far west was alone or especially afflicted by the terror that was over the land. They tell me that in the villages about Dartmoor the stout Devonshire hearts sank as men's hearts used to sink in the time of plague and pestilence. There was horror, too, about the Norfolk Broads, and far up by Perth no one would venture on the path that leads by Scone to the wooded heights above the Tay. And in the industrial districts : I met a man by chance one day in an odd London corner who spoke with horror of what a friend had told him.

" ' Ask no questions, Ned,' he says to me, ' but I tell yow a' was in Bairnigan t'other day, and a' met a pal who'd seen three hundred coffins going out of a works not far from there.' "

And then the ship that hovered outside the mouth of the Thames with all sails set and beat to and fro in the wind, and never answered any hail, and showed no light ! The forts shot at her and brought down one of the masts, but she went suddenly about with a change of wind under what sail still stood, and then veered down Channel, and drove ashore at last on the sandbanks and pinewoods of Arcachon, and not a man alive on her, but only rattling heaps of bones ! That last voyage of the *Semiramis* would be something horribly worth telling ; but I only heard it at a distance as a yarn, and only believed it because it squared with other things that I knew for certain.

This, then, is my point ; I have written of the terror as it fell on Meirion, simply because I have had opportunities of getting close there to what really happened. Third or fourth or fifth hand in the other places ; but round about Porth and Merthyr Tegveth I have spoken with people who have seen the tracks of the terror with their own eyes.

Well, I have said that the people of that far western county realized, not only that death was abroad in their quiet lanes and on their peaceful hills, but that for some reason it was to be kept all secret. Newspapers might not print any news of it, the very juries summoned to investigate it were allowed to investigate nothing. And so they concluded that this veil of secrecy must somehow be connected with the war ; and from this position it was not a long way to a further inference : that the murderers of innocent men and women and children were either Germans or agents of Germany. It would be just like the Huns, everybody agreed, to think out such a devilish scheme as this ; and they always thought out their schemes beforehand. They hoped to seize Paris in a few weeks, but when they were beaten on the Marne they had their trenches on the Aisne ready to fall back on : it had all been prepared years before the war. And so, no doubt, they had devised this terrible plan against

England in case they could not beat us in open fight : there were people ready, very likely, all over the country, who were prepared to murder and destroy everywhere as soon as they got the word. In this way the Germans intended to sow terror throughout England and fill our hearts with panic and dismay, hoping so to weaken their enemy at home that he would lose all heart over the war abroad. It was the Zeppelin notion, in another form ; they were committing these horrible and mysterious outrages thinking that we should be frightened out of our wits.

It all seemed plausible enough ; Germany had by this time perpetrated so many horrors and had so excelled in devilish ingenuities that no abomination seemed too abominable to be probable, or too ingeniously wicked to be beyond the tortuous malice of the Hun. But then came the questions as to who the agents of this terrible design were, as to where they lived, as to how they contrived to move unseen from field to field, from lane to lane. All sorts of fantastic attempts were made to answer these questions ; but it was felt that they remained unanswered. Some suggested that the murderers landed from submarines, or flew from hiding places on the West Coast of Ireland, coming and going by night ; but there were seen to be flagrant impossibilities in both these suggestions. Everybody agreed that the evil work was no doubt the work of Germany ; but nobody could begin to guess how it was done. Somebody at the Club asked Remnant for his theory.

" My theory," said that ingenious person, " is that human progress is simply a long march from one inconceivable to another. Look at that airship of ours that came over Porth yesterday : ten years ago that would have been an inconceivable sight. Take the steam engine, take printing, take the theory of gravitation : they were all inconceivable till somebody thought of them. So it is, no doubt, with this infernal dodgery that we're talking about : the Huns have found it out, and we haven't ; and there you are. We can't conceive how these poor people have been murdered, because the method's inconceivable to us."

The club listened with some awe to this high argument. After Remnant had gone, one member said :

" Wonderful man, that." " Yes," said Dr. Lewis. " He was asked whether he

knew something. And his reply really
amounted to ' No, I don't.' But I have
never heard it better put.''

It was, I suppose, at about this time
when the people were puzzling their heads
as to the secret method used by the Germans
or their agents to accomplish their crimes
that a very singular circumstance became
known to a few of the Porth people. It
related to the murder of the Williams
family on the Highway in front of their
cottage door. I do not know that I have
made it plain that the old Roman road
called the Highway follows the course of a
long, steep hill that goes steadily westward
till it slants down and droops towards the
sea. On either side of the road the ground
falls away, here into deep shadowy woods,
here to high pastures, now and again
into a field of corn, but for the most part
into the wild and broken land that is
characteristic of Arfon. The fields are long
and narrow, stretching up the steep hillside ;
they fall into sudden dips and hollows, a
well springs up in the midst of one and a
grove of ash and thorn bends over it, shad-
ing it ; and beneath it the ground is thick
with reeds and rushes. And then may

come on either side of such a field territories glistening with the deep growth of bracken, and rough with gorse and rugged with thickets of blackthorn, green lichen hanging strangely from the branches ; such are the lands on either side of the Highway.

Now on the lower slopes of it, beneath the Williams's cottage, some three or four fields down the hill, there is a military camp. The place has been used as a camp for many years, and lately the site has been extended and huts have been erected. But a considerable number of the men were under canvas here in the summer of 1915.

On the night of the Highway murder this camp, as it appeared afterwards, was the scene of the extraordinary panic of the horses.

A good many men in the camp were asleep in their tents soon after 9.30, when the Last Post was sounded. They woke up in panic. There was a thundering sound on the steep hillside above them, and down upon the tents came half a dozen horses, mad with fright, trampling the canvas, trampling the men, bruising dozens of them and killing two.

Everything was in wild confusion, men groaning and screaming in the darkness, struggling with the canvas and the twisted ropes, shouting out, some of them, raw lads enough, that the Germans had landed, others wiping the blood from their eyes, a few, roused suddenly from heavy sleep, hitting out at one another, officers coming up at the double roaring out orders to the sergeants, a party of soldiers who were just returning to camp from the village seized with fright at what they could scarcely see or distinguish, at the wildness of the shouting and cursing and groaning that they could not understand, bolting out of the camp again and racing for their lives back to the village : everything in the maddest confusion of wild disorder.

Some of the men had seen the horses galloping down the hill as if terror itself was driving them. They scattered off into the darkness, and somehow or another found their way back in the night to their pasture above the camp. They were grazing there peacefully in the morning, and the only sign of the panic of the night before was the mud they had scattered all over themselves as they pelted through a patch of wet ground. The farmer said they were as quiet a lot as any in Meirion ; he could make nothing of it.

" Indeed," he said, " I believe they must have seen the devil himself to be in such a fright as that : save the people ! "

Now all this was kept as quiet as might be at the time when it happened ; it became known to the men of the Porth Club in the days when they were discussing the difficult question of the German outrages, as the murders were commonly called. And this wild stampede of the farm horses was held by some to be evidence of the extraordinary and unheard-of character of the dreadful agency that was at work. One of the members of the club had been told by an officer who was in the camp at the time of the panic that the horses that came charging down were in a perfect fury of fright, that he had never seen horses in such a state, and so there was endless speculation as to the nature of the sight or the sound that had driven half a dozen quiet beasts into raging madness.

Then, in the middle of this talk, two or three other incidents, quite as odd and incomprehensible, came to be known, borne on chance trickles of gossip that came into the towns from outland farms, or were

carried by cottagers tramping into Porth
on market-day with a fowl or two and eggs
and garden stuff ; scraps and fragments of
talk gathered by servants from the country
folk and repeated to their mistresses. And
in such ways it came out that up at Plas
Newydd there had been a terrible business
over swarming the bees ; they had turned
as wild as wasps and much more savage.
They had come about the people who were
taking the swarm like a cloud. They settled
on one man's face so that you could not
see the flesh for the bees crawling all over
it, and they had stung him so badly that
the doctor did not know whether he would
get over it, and they had chased a girl who
had come out to see the swarming, and
settled on her and stung her to death. Then
they had gone off to a brake below the farm
and got into a hollow tree there, and it
was not safe to go near it, for they would
come out at you by day or by night.

And much the same thing had happened,
it seemed, at three or four farms and cottages where bees were kept. And there were
stories, hardly so clear or so credible, of
sheep dogs, mild and trusted beasts, turning as savage as wolves and injuring the
farm boys in a horrible manner—in one case

it was said with fatal results. It was certainly true that old Mrs. Owen's favourite Brahma-Dorking cock had gone mad ; she came into Porth one Saturday morning with her face and her neck all bound up and plastered. She had gone out to her bit of a field to feed the poultry the night before, and the bird had flown at her and attacked her most savagely, inflicting some very nasty wounds before she could beat it off.

" There was a stake handy, lucky for me," she said, " and I did beat him and beat him till the life was out of him. But what is come to the world, whatever ? "

Now Remnant, the man of theories, was also a man of extreme leisure. It was understood that he had succeeded to amdle means when he was quite a young man, and after tasting the savours of the law, as it were, for half a dozen terms at the board of the Middle Temple, he had decided that it would be senseless to bother himself with passing examinations for a profession which he had not the faintest intention of practising. So he turned a deaf ear to the call of " Manger " ringing through the Temple Courts, and set himself out to potter amiably through the world. He had pot-

tered all over Europe, he had looked at
Africa, and had even put his head in at the
door of the East, on a trip which included
the Greek isles and Constantinople. Now,
getting into the middle fifties, he had
settled at Porth for the sake, as he said,
of the Gulf Stream and the fuchsia hedges,
and pottered over his books and his theories
and the local gossip. He was no more
brutal than the general public, which
revels in the details of mysterious crime ;
but it must be said that the terror, black
though it was, was a boon to him. He
peered and investigated and poked about
with the relish of a man to whose life a
new zest has been added. He listened
attentively to the strange tales of bees and
dogs and poultry that came into Porth with
the country baskets of butter, rabbits, and
green peas ; and he evolved at last a most
extraordinary theory.

Full of this discovery, as he thought it,
he went one night to see Dr. Lewis and take
his view of the matter.

" I want to talk to you," said Remnant
to the doctor, " about what I have called,
provisionally, the Z Ray."

# CHAPTER V

DR. LEWIS, smiling indulgently, and quite prepared for some monstrous piece of theorizing, led Remnant into the room that overlooked the terraced garden and the sea.

The doctor's house, though it was only a ten minutes' walk from the centre of the town, seemed remote from all other habitations. The drive to it from the road came through a deep grove of trees and a dense shrubbery, trees were about the house on either side, mingling with neighbouring groves, and below, the garden fell down, terrace by green terrace, to wild growth, a twisted path amongst red rocks, and at last to the yellow sand of a little cove. The room to which the doctor took Remnant looked over these terraces and across the water to the dim boundaries of the bay. It had French windows that were thrown wide open, and the two men sat in the soft light of the lamp—this was before the days of severe lighting regulations in the far west —and enjoyed the sweet odours and the sweet vision of the summer evening. Then Remnant began :

" I suppose, Lewis, you've heard these extraordinary stories of bees and dogs and things that have been going about lately ? "

" Certainly I have heard them. I was called in at Plas Newydd, and treated Thomas Trevor, who's only just out of danger, by the way. I certified for the poor child, Mary Trevor. She was dying when I got to the place. There was no doubt she was stung to death by bees, and I believe there were other very similar cases at Llantarnam and Morwen ; none fatal, I think. What about them ? "

" Well : then there are the stories of good-tempered old sheepdogs turning wicked and ' savaging ' children ? "

" Quite so. I haven't seen any of these cases professionally ; but I believe the stories are accurate enough."

" And the old woman assaulted by her own poultry ? "

" That's perfectly true. Her daughter put some stuff of their own concoction on her face and neck, and then she came to me. The wounds seemed going all right, so I told her to continue the treatment, whatever it might be."

" Very good," said Mr. Remnant. He spoke now with an italic impressiveness. *"Don't you see the link between all this and the horrible things that have been happening about here for the last month ?* "

Lewis stared at Remnant in amazement. He lifted his red eyebrows and lowered them in a kind of scowl. His speech showed traces of his native accent.

" Great burning ! " he exclaimed. "What on earth are you getting at now ? It is madness. Do you mean to tell me that you think there is some connexion between a swarm or two of bees that have turned nasty, a cross dog, and a wicked old barn-door cock and these poor people that have been pitched over the cliffs and hammered to death on the road ? There's no sense in it, you know."

" I am strongly inclined to believe that there is a great deal of sense in it," replied Remnant, with extreme calmness. " Look here, Lewis, I saw you grinning the other day at the club when I was telling the fellows that in my opinion all these outrages had been committed, certainly by the Germans, but by some method of which we have no conception. But what I meant to say when I talked about inconceivables was just this : that the Williams's and the rest of them have been killed in some way that's not in theory at all, not in our theory, at all events, some way we've not contemplated, not thought of for an instant. Do you see my point ? "

" Well, in a sort of way. You mean there's an absolute originality in the method ? I suppose that is so. But what next ? "

Remnant seemed to hesitate, partly from a sense of the portentous nature of what he was about to say, partly from a sort of half-unwillingness to part with so profound a secret.

" Well," he said, " you will allow that we have two sets of phenomena of a very extraordinary kind occurring at the same time. Don't you think that it's only reasonable to connect the two sets with one another."

" So the philosopher of Tenterden steeple and the Goodwin Sands thought, certainly," said Lewis. " But what is the connexion ? Those poor folks on the Highway weren't stung by bees or worried by a dog. And horses don't throw people over cliffs or stifle them in marshes."

" No ; I never meant to suggest anything so absurd. It is evident to me that in all these cases of animals turning suddenly savage the cause has been terror, panic, fear. The horses that went charging into the camp were mad with fright, we know. And I say that in the other instances we have been discussing the cause was the same. The creatures were exposed to an infection of fear, and a frightened beast or bird or insect uses its weapons, whatever they may be. If, for example, there had been anybody with those horses when they took their panic they would have lashed out at him with their heels."

" Yes, I dare say that that is so. Well."

" Well ; my belief is that the Germans have made an extraordinary discovery. I have called it the Z Ray. You know that the ether is merely an hypothesis ; we have to suppose that it's there to account for the passage of the Marconi current from one place to another. Now, suppose that there is a psychic æther as well as a material æther, suppose that it is possible to direct irresistable impulses across this medium, suppose that these impulses are towards murder or suicide ; then I think that you have an explanation of the terrible series of events that have been happening in Meirion for the last few weeks. And it is quite clear to my mind that the horses and the other creatures have been exposed to this Z Ray, and that it has produced on them the effect of terror, with ferocity as the result of terror. Now what do you say to that ? Telepathy, you know, is well established ; so is hypnotic suggestion. You have only to look in the ' Encyclopædia Britannica ' to see that, and suggestion is so strong in some cases as to be an irresistible imperative. Now don't you feel that putting telepathy and suggestion together, as it were, you have more than the elements of what I call the Z Ray ? I feel myself that I have more to go on in making my hypothesis than the inventor of the steam-engine had in making his hypothesis when he saw the lid of the kettle bobbing up and down. What do you say ? "

Dr. Lewis made no answer. He was watching the growth of a new, unknown tree in his garden.

The doctor made no answer to Remnant's question. For one thing, Remnant was profuse in his eloquence—he has been rigidly condensed in this history—and Lewis was tired of the sound of his voice. For another thing, he found the Z Ray theory almost too extravagant to be bearable, wild enough to tear patience to tatters. And

then as the tedious argument continued
Lewis became conscious that there was
something strange about the night.

It was a dark summer night. The moon
was old and faint, above the Dragon's Head
across the bay, and the air was very still.
It was so still that Lewis had noted that
not a leaf stirred on the very tip of a high
tree that stood out against the sky ; and yet
he knew that he was listening to some
sound that he could not determine or de-
fine. It was not the wind in the leaves, it
was not the gentle wash of the water of the
sea against the rocks ; that latter sound he
could distinguish quite easily. But there
was something else. It was scarcely a
sound ; it was as if the air air itself trembled
and fluttered, as the air trembles in a
church when they open the great pedal
pipes of the organ.

The doctor listened intently. It was not
an illusion, the sound was not in his own
head, as he had suspected for a moment ;
but for the life of him he could not make
out whence it came or what it was. He
gazed down into the night over the terraces
of his garden, now sweet with the scent of
the flowers of the night ; tried to peer over
the tree-tops across the sea towards the

Dragon's Head. It struck him suddenly
that this strange fluttering vibration of the
air might be the noise of a distant aeroplane
or airship ; there was not the usual droning
hum, but this sound might be caused by a
new type of engine. A new type of engine ?
Possibly it was an enemy airship ; their
range, it had been said, was getting longer ;
and Lewis was just going to call Remnant's
attention to the sound, to its possible cause,
and to the possible danger that might be
hovering over them, when he saw something
that caught his breath and his heart with
wild amazement and a touch of terror.

He had been staring upward into the
sky, and, about to speak to Remnant, he
had let his eyes drop for an instant. He
looked down towards the trees in the garden,
and saw with utter astonishment that
one had changed its shape in the few hours
that had passed since the setting of the
sun. There was a thick grove of ilexes
bordering the lowest terrace, and above
them rose one tall pine, spreading its head
of sparse, dark branches dark against the
sky.

As Lewis glanced down over the terraces
he saw that the tall pine tree was no longer
there. In its place there rose above the

ilexes what might have been a greater ilex ; there was the blackness of a dense growth of foliage rising like a broad and far-spreading and rounded cloud over the lesser trees.

Here, then was a sight wholly incredible, impossible. It is doubtful whether the process of the human mind in such a case has ever been analysed and registered ; it is doubtful whether it ever can be registered. It is hardly fair to bring in the mathematician, since he deals with absolute truth (so far as mortality can conceive absolute truth) ; but how would a mathematician feel if he were suddenly confronted with a two-sided triangle ? I suppose he would instantly become a raging madman ; and Lewis, staring wide-eyed and wild-eyed at a dark and spreading tree which his own experience informed him was not there, felt for an instant that shock which should affront us all when we first realize the intolerable antinomy of Achilles and the Tortoise. Common sense tells us that Achilles will flash past the tortoise almost with the speed of the lightning ; the inflexible truth of mathematics assures us that till the earth boils and the heavens cease to endure the Tortoise must still be in advance ; and thereupon we should, in common decency, go mad. We do not go mad, because, by special grace, we are certified that, in the final court of appeal, all science is a lie, even the highest science of all ; and so we simply grin at Achilles and the Tortoise, as we grin at Darwin, deride Huxley, and laugh at Herbert Spencer.

Dr. Lewis did not grin. He glared into the dimness of the night, at the great spreading tree that he knew could not be there. And as he gazed he saw that what at first appeared the dense blackness of foliage was freeted and starred with wonderful appearances of lights and colours.

Afterwards he said to me : "I remember thinking to myself : 'Look here, I am not delirious ; my temperature is perfectly normal. I am not drunk ; I only had a pint of Graves with my dinner, over three hours ago. I have not eaten any poisonous fungus ; I have not taken *Anhelonium Lewinii* experimentally. So, now then ! What is happening ? ' "

The night had gloomed over ; clouds obscured the faint moon and the misty stars. Lewis rose, with some kind of warning and inhibiting gesture to Remnant, who, he was conscious was gaping at him in astonish-

E

ment. He walked to the open French window, and took a pace forward on to the path outside, and looked, very intently, at the dark shape of the tree, down below the sloping garden, above the washing of the waves. He shaded the light of the lamp behind him by holding his hands on each side of his eyes.

The mass of the tree—the tree that couldn't be there—stood out against the sky, but not so clearly, now that the clouds had rolled up. Its edges, the limits of its leafage, were not so distinct. Lewis thought that he could detect some sort of quivering movement in it ; though the air was at a dead calm. It was a night on which one might hold up a lighted match and watch it burn without any wavering or inclination of the flame.

" You know," said Lewis, " how a bit of burnt paper will sometimes hang over the coals before it goes up the chimney, and little worms of fire will shoot through it. It was like that, if you should be standing some distance away. Just threads and hairs of yellow light I saw, and specks and sparks of fire, and then a twinkling of a ruby no bigger than a pin point, and a green wandering in the black, as if an emerald were crawling, and then little veins of deep blue. ' Woe is me ! ' I said to myself in Welsh, ' What is all this colour and burning ? '

" And, then, at that very moment there came a thundering rap at the door of the room inside, and there was my man telling me that I was wanted directly up at the Garth, as old Mr. Trevor Williams had been taken very bad. I knew his heart was not worth much, so I had to go off directly, and leave Remnant to make what he could of it all."

# CHAPTER VI

Dr. Lewis was kept some time at the Garth. It was past twelve when he got back to his house. He went quickly to the room that overlooked the garden and the sea and threw open the French window and peered into the darkness. There, dim indeed against the dim sky but unmistakable, was the tall pine with its sparse branches, high above the dense growth of the ilex trees. The strange boughs which had amazed him had vanished ; there was no appearance now of colours or of fires.

He drew his chair up to the open window and sat there gazing and wondering far into the night, till brightness came upon the sea and sky, and the forms of the trees in the garden grew clear and evident. He went up to his bed at last filled with a great perplexity, still asking questions to which there was no answer.

The doctor did not say anything about the strange tree to Remnant. When they next met, Lewis said that he had thought there was a man hiding amongst the bushes —this in explanation of that warning gesture he had used, and of his going out into the garden and staring into the night. He concealed the truth because he dreaded the Remnant doctrine that would undoubtedly be produced ; indeed, he hoped that he had heard the last of the theory of the Z Ray. But Remnant firmly reopened this subject.

" We were interrupted just as I was putting my case to you," he said. " And to sum it all up, it amounts to this : that the Huns have made one of the great leaps of science. They are sending ' suggestions ' (which amount to irresistible commands) over here, and the persons affected are seized with suicidal or homicidal mania. The people who were killed by falling over the cliffs or into the quarry probably committed suicide ; and so with the man and boy who were found in the bog. As to the Highway case, you remember that Thomas Evans said that he stopped and talked to Williams on the night of the murder. In my opinion Evans was the murderer. He came under the influence of the Ray, became a homicidal maniac in an instant, snatched Williams's spade from his hand and killed him and the others."

" The bodies were found by me on the road."

" It is possible that the first impact of

the Ray produces violent nervous excite-
ment, which would manifest itself exter-
nally. Williams might have called to his
wife to come and see what was the matter
with Evans. The children would naturally
follow their mother. It seems to me
simple. And as for the animals—the
horses, dogs, and so forth, they as I say,
were no doubt panic-stricken by the Ray,
and hence driven to frenzy."

"Why should Evans have murdered
Williams instead of Williams murdering
Evans? Why should the impact of the
Ray affect one and not the other?"

"Why does one man react violently to a
certain drug, while it makes no impression
on another man? Why is A able to drink a
bottle of whisky and remain sober, while B
is turned into something very like a lunatic
after he has drunk three glasses?"

"It is a question of idiosyncrasy," said
the doctor.

"Is idiosyncrasy Greek for 'I don't
know'?" asked Remnant.

"Not at all," said Lewis, smiling blandly.
"I mean that in some diatheses whisky
—as you have mentioned whisky—appears
not to be pathogenic, or at all events not
immediately pathogenic. In other cases, as

you very justly observed, there seems to be a very marked cachexia associated with the exhibition of the spirit in question, even in comparatively small doses."

Under this cloud of professional verbiage Lewis escaped from the Club and from Remnant. He did not want to hear any more about that dreadful Ray, because he felt sure that the Ray was all nonsense. But asking himself why he felt this certitude in the matter he had to confess that he didn't know. An aeroplane he reflected, was all nonsense before it was made ; and he remembered talking in the early nineties to a friend of his about the newly discovered X Rays. The friend laughed incredulously, evidently didn't believe a word of it, till Lewis told him that there was an article on the subject in the current number of the *Saturday Review* ; whereupon the unbeliever said, " Oh, is that so ? Oh, really. I *see*," and was converted to the X Ray faith on the spot. Lewis, remembering this talk, marvelled at the strange processes of the human mind, its illogical and yet all-compelling *ergos*, and wondered whether he himself was only waiting for an article on the Z Ray in the *Saturday Review* to become a devout believer in the doctrine of Remnant.

But he wondered with far more fervour
as to the extraordinary thing he had seen in
in his own garden with his own eyes. The tree
that changed all its shape for an hour or two
of the night, the growth of strange boughs,
the apparition of secret fires among them, the
sparkling of emerald and ruby lights : how
could one fail to be afraid with great amazement at the thought of such a mystery ?

Dr. Lewis's thoughts were distracted
from the incredible adventure of the tree
by the visit of his sister and her husband.
Mr. and Mrs. Merritt lived in a well-known
manufacturing town of the Midlands, which
was now, of course, a centre of munition
work.  On the day of their arrival at
Porth, Mrs. Merritt, who was tired after
the long, hot journey, went to bed early,
and Merritt and Lewis went into the room
by the garden for their talk and tobacco.
They spoke of the year that had passed
since their last meeting, of the weary
dragging of the war, of friends that had
perished in it, of the hopelessness of an
early ending of all this misery. Lewis said
nothing of the terror that was on the land.
One does not greet a tired man who is come
to a quiet, sunny place for relief from black

smoke and work and worry with a tale of horror. Indeed, the doctor saw that his brother-in-law looked far from well. And he seemed " jumpy " ; there was an occasional twitch of his mouth that Lewis did not like at all.

" Well," said the doctor, after an interval of silence and port wine, " I am glad to see you here again. Porth always suits you. I don't think you're looking quite up to your usual form. But three weeks of Meirion air will do wonders."

" Well, I hope it will," said the other. " I am not up to the mark. Things are not going well at Midlingham."

" Business is all right isn't it ? "

" Yes. Business is all right. But there are other things that are all wrong. We are living under a reign of terror. It comes to that."

" What on earth do you mean ? "

" Well, I suppose I may tell you what I know. It's not much. I didn't dare write it. But do you know that at every one of the munition works in Midlingham and all about it there's a guard of soldiers with drawn bayonets and loaded rifles day and night ? Men with bombs, too. And machine-guns at the big factories."

" German spies ? "

" You don't want Lewis guns to fight spies with. Nor bombs. Nor a platoon of men. I woke up last night. It was the machine-gun at Benington's Army Motor Works. Firing like fury. And then bang ! bang ! bang ! That was the hand bombs."

" But what against ? "

" Nobody knows."

" Nobody knows what is happening," Merritt repeated, and he went on to describe the bewilderment and terror that hung like a cloud over the great industrial city in the Midlands, how the feeling of concealment, of some intolerable secret danger that must not be named, was worst of all.

" A young fellow I know," he said, " was on short leave the other day from the front, and he spent it with his people at Belmont —that's about four miles out of Midlingham, you know. ' Thank God,' he said to me, ' I am going back to-morrow. It's no good saying that the Wipers salient is nice, because it isn't. But it's a damned sight better than this. At the front you know what you're up against, anyhow.' At Midlingham everybody has the feeling that we're up against something awful and we don't

know what ; it's that that makes people inclined to whisper.  There's terror in the air."

Merritt made a sort of picture of the
great town cowering in its fear of an
unknown danger.

" People are afraid to go about alone at
nights in the outskirts.  They make up
parties at the stations to go home together
if it's anything like dark, or if there are
any lonely bits on their way."

" But why ?  I don't understand.  What
are they afraid of ? "

" Well, I told you about my being woke
up the other night with the machine-guns
at the motor works rattling away, and the
bombs exploding and making the most
terrible noise.  That sort of thing alarms
one, you know.  It's only natural."

" Indeed, it must be very terrifying.
You mean, then, there is a general nervous-
ness about, a vague sort of apprehension that
makes people inclined to herd together ? "

" There's that, and there's more.  People
have gone out that have never come back.
There were a couple of men in the train to
Holme, arguing about the quickest way to
get to Northend, a sort of outlying part of
Holme where they both lived.  They
argued all the way out of Midlingham, one

saying that the high road was the quickest though it was the longest way. ' It's the quickest going because it's the cleanest going,' he said.

The other chap fancied a short cut across the fields, by the canal. ' It's half the distance,' he kept on. ' Yes, if you don't lose your way,' said the other. Well, it appears they put an even half-crown on it, and each was to try his own way when they got out of the train. It was arranged that they were to meet at the ' Waggon ' in Northend. ' I shall be at the ' Waggon ' first,' said the man who believed in the short cut, and with that he climbed over the stile and made off across the fields. It wasn't late enough to be really dark, and a lot of them thought he might win the stakes. But he never turned up at the Waggon— or anywhere else for the matter of that."

" What happened to him ? "

" He was found lying on his back in the middle of a field—some way from the path. He was dead. The doctors said he'd been suffocated. Nobody knows how. Then there have been other cases. We whisper about them at Midlingham, but we're afraid to speak out."

Lewis was ruminating all this pro-

foundly. Terror in Meirion and terror far
away in the heart of England ; but at Midlingham, so far as he could gather from
these stories of soldiers on guard, of
crackling machine-guns, it was a case of an
organized attack on the munitioning of the
army. He felt that he did not know enough
to warrant his deciding that the terror of
Meirion and of Stratfordshire were one.

Then Merritt began again : .

" There's a queer story going about, when
the door's shut and the curtain's drawn,
that is, as to a place right out in the country
over the other side of Midlingham ; on the
opposite side to Dunwich. They've built
one of the new factories out there, a great
red brick town of sheds they tell me it is,
with a tremendous chimney. It's not been
finished more than a month or six weeks.
They plumped it down right in the middle
of the fields, by the line, and they're building huts for the workers as fast as they can
but up to the present the men are billeted
all about, up and down the line.

" About two hundred yards from this
place there's an old footpath, leading from
the station and the main road up to a small
hamlet on the hillside. Part of the way
this path goes by a pretty large wood, most

of it thick undergrowth. I should think there must be twenty acres of wood, more or less. As it happens, I used this path once long ago ; and I can tell you it's a black place of nights.

" A man had to go this way one night. He got along all right till he came to the wood. And then he said his heart dropped out of his body. It was awful to hear the noises in that wood. Thousands of men were in it, he swears that. It was full of rustling, and pattering of feet trying to go dainty, and the crack of dead boughs lying on the ground as someone trod on them, and swishing of the grass, and some sort of chattering speech going on, that sounded, so he said, as if the dead sat in their bones and talked ! He ran for his life, anyhow ; across fields, over hedges, through brooks. He must have run, by his tale, ten miles out of his way before he got home to his wife, and beat at the door, and broke in, and bolted it behind him."

" There is something rather alarming about any wood at night," said Dr. Lewis.

Merritt shrugged his shoulders.

" People say that the Germans have landed, and that they are hiding in underground places all over the country."

# CHAPTER VII

Lewis gasped for a moment, silent in contemplation of the magnificence of rumour. The Germans already landed, hiding underground, striking by night, secretly, terribly, at the power of England! Here was a conception which made the myth of " The Russians " a paltry fable ; before which the Legend of Mons was an ineffectual thing.

It was monstrous. And yet——

He looked steadily at Merritt ; a square-headed, black-haired, solid sort of man. He had symptons of nerves about him for the moment, certainly, but one could not wonder at that, whether the tales he told were true, or whether he merely believed them to be true. Lewis had known his brother-in-law for twenty years or more, and had always found him a sure man in his own small world. " But then," said the doctor to himself, " those men, if they once get out of the ring of that little world of theirs, they are lost. Those are the men that believed in Madame Blavatsky."

" Well," he said, " what do you think yourself ? The Germans landed and hiding somewhere about the country : there's something extravagant in the notion, isn't there ? "

" I don't know what to think. You can't get over the facts. There are the soldiers with their rifles and their guns at the works all over Stratfordshire, and those guns go off. I told you I'd heard them. Then who are the soldiers shooting at ? That's what we ask ourselves at Midlingham."

" Quite so ; I quite understand. It's an extraordinary state of things."

" It's more than extraordinary ; it's an awful state of things. It's terror in the dark, and there's nothing worse than that. As that young fellow I was telling you about said, 'At the front you do know what you're up against."

" And people really believe that a number of Germans have somehow got over to England and have hid themselves underground ? "

" People say they've got a new kind of poison-gas. Some think that they dig underground places and make the gas there, and lead it by secret pipes into the shops ; others say that they throw gas bombs into the factories. It must be worse than anything they've used in France, from what the authorities say."

" The authorities ? Do *they* admit that there are Germans in hiding about Midlingham ? "

" No. They call it ' explosions.' But we know it isn't explosions. We know in the Midlands what an explosion sounds like and looks like. And we know that the people killed in these ' explosions' are put into their coffins in the works. Their own relations are not allowed to see them."

" And so you believe in the German theory ? "

" If I do, it's because one must believe in something. Some say they've seen the gas. I heard that a man living in Dunwich saw it one night like a black cloud with sparks of fire in it floating over the tops of the trees by Dunwich Common."

The light of an ineffable amazement came into Lewis's eyes. The night of Remnant's visit, the trembling vibration of the air, the dark tree that had grown in his garden since the setting of the sun, the strange leafage that was starred with burning, with emerald and ruby fires, and all vanished away when he returned from his visit to the Garth ; and such a leafage had appeared as a burning cloud far in the heart of England : what intolerable mys-

F

tery, what tremendous doom was signified in this? But one thing was clear and certain : that the terror of Meirion was also the terror of the Midlands.

Lewis made up his mind most firmly that if possible all this should be kept from his brother-in-law. Merritt had come to Porth as to a city of refuge from the horrors of Midlingham ; if it could be managed he should be spared the knowledge that the cloud of terror had gone before him and hung black over the western land. Lewis passed the port and said in an even voice :

" Very strange, indeed ; a black cloud with sparks of fire ? "

" I can't answer for it, you know ; it's only a rumour."

" Just so ; and you think or you're inclined to think that this and all the rest you've told me is to be put down to the hidden Germans ? "

" As I say ; because one must think something.

" I quite see your point. No doubt, if it's true, it's the most awful blow that has even been dealt at any nation in the whole history of man. The enemy established in our vitals ! But is it possible, after all ? How could it have been worked ? "

Merritt told Lewis how it had been worked, or rather, how people said it had been worked. The idea, he said, was that this was a part, and a most important part, of the great German plot to destroy England and the British Empire.

The scheme had been prepared years ago, some thought soon after the Franco-Prussian War. Moltke had seen that the invasion of England (in the ordinary sense of the term invasion) presented very great difficulties. The matter was constantly in discussion in the inner military and high political circles, and the general trend of opinion in these quarters was that at the best, the invasion of England would involve Germany in the gravest difficulties, and leave France in the position of the *tertius gaudens*. This was the state of affairs when a very high Prussian personage was approached by the Swedish professor, Huvelius.

Thus Merritt, and here I would say in parenthesis that this Huvelius was by all accounts an extraordinary man. Considered personally and apart from his writings he would appear to have been a most amiable individual. He was richer than the generality of Swedes, certainly far richer than

the average university professor in Sweden.
But his shabby, green frock-coat, and his
battered, furry hat were notorious in the
university town where he lived. No one
laughed, because it was well known that
Professor Huvelius spent every penny of
his private means and a large portion of
his official stipend on works of kindness and
charity. He hid his head in a garret, someone said, in order that others might be able
to swell on the first floor. It was told of
him that he restricted himself to a diet of
dry bread and coffee for a month, in order
that a poor woman of the streets, dying of
consumption, might enjoy luxuries in
hospital.

And this was the man who wrote the
treatise " De Facinore Humano " ; to prove
the infinite corruption of the human race.

Oddly enough, Professor Huvelius wrote
the most cynical book in the world—Hobbes
preaches rosy sentimentalism in comparison
—with the very highest motives. He held
that a very large part of human misery,
misadventure, and sorrow was due to the
false convention that the heart of man was
naturally and in the main well disposed and
kindly, if not exactly righteous. " Mur
derers, thieves, assassins, violators, and all

the host of the abominable," he says in one passage, " are created by the false pretence and foolish credence of human virtue. A lion in a cage is a fierce beast, indeed ; but what will he be if we declare him to be a lamb and open the doors of his den ? Who will be guilty of the deaths of the men, women and children whom he will surely devour, save those who unlocked the cage ?" And he goes on to show that kings and the rulers of the peoples could decrease the sum of human misery to a vast extent by acting on the doctrine of human wickedness. " War," he declares, " which is one of the worst of evils, will always continue to exist. But a wise king will desire a brief war rather than a lengthy one, a short evil rather than a long evil. And this not from the benignity of his heart towards his enemies, for we have seen that the human heart is naturally malignant, but because he desires to conquer, and to conquer easily, without a great expenditure of men or of treasure, knowing that if he can accomplish this feat his people will love him and his crown will be secure. So he will wage brief victorious wars, and not only spare his own nation, but the nation of the enemy, since in a short war the loss is less on both sides than in a

long war. And so from evil will come
good."

And how, asks Huvelius, are such wars
to be waged ? The wise prince, he replies,
will begin by assuming the enemy to be
infinitely corruptible and infinitely stupid,
since stupidity and corruption are the chief
characteristics of man. So the prince will
make himself friends in the very councils
of his enemy, and also amongst the populace, bribing the wealthy by proffering to
them the opportunity of still greater wealth,
and winning the poor by swelling words.
" For, contrary to the common opinion, it is
the wealthy who are greedy of wealth ;
while the populace are to be gained by talking to them about liberty, their unknown
god. And so much are they enchanted
by the words liberty, freedom, and such like,
that the wise can go to the poor, rob them
of what little they have, dismiss them
with a hearty kick, and win their hearts
and their votes for ever, if only they will
assure them that the treatment which
they have received is called liberty."

Guided by these principles, says Huvelius, the wise prince will entrench himself
in the country that he desires to conquer ;
" nay, with but little trouble, he may

actually and literally throw his garrisons into the heart of the enemy country before war has begun.''

This is a long and tiresome parenthesis ; but it is necessary as explaining the long tale which Merritt told his brotheri-in-law, he having received it from some magnate of the Midlands, who had travelled in Germany. It is probable that the story was suggested in the first place by the passage from Huvelius which I have just quoted.

Merritt knew nothing of the real Huvelius, who was all but a saint ; he thought of the Swedish professor as a monster of iniquity, '' worse,'' as he said, '' than Neech ''—meaning, no doubt, Nietzsche.

So he told the story of how Huvelius had sold his plan to the Germans ; a plan for filling England with German soldiers. Land was to be bought in certain suitable and well-considered places, Englishmen were to be bought as the apparent owners of such land, and secret excavations were to be made, till the country was literally undermined. A subterranean Germany, in fact, was to be dug under selected districts of England ; there were to be great caverns, underground cities, well drained, well ven-

tilated, supplied with water, and in these
places vast stores both of food and of munitions were to be accumulated, year after
year, till " the Day " dawned. And then,
warned in time, the secret garrison would
leave shops, hotels, offices, villas, and
vanish underground, ready to begin
their work of bleeding England at the
heart.

" That's what Henson told me," said
Merritt at the end of his long story. " Hen-
son, head of the Buckley Iron and Steel
Syndicate. He has been a lot in Germany."

" Well," said Lewis, " of course, it may
be so. If it is so, it is terrible beyond
words."

Indeed, he found something horribly
plausible in the story. It was an extraordinary plan, of course ; an unheard of
scheme ; but it did not seem impossible. It
was the Trojan Horse on a gigantic scale ;
indeed, he reflected, the story of the horse
with the warriors concealed within it which
was dragged into the heart of Troy by the
deluded Trojans themselves might be taken
as a prophetic parable of what had happened
to England—if Henson's theory were well
founded. And this theory certainly squared
with what one had heard of German pre-

parations in Belgium and in France : emplacements for guns ready for the invader, German manufactories which were really German forts on Belgian soil, the caverns by the Aisne made ready for the cannon ; indeed, Lewis thought he remembered something about suspicious concrete tennis-courts on the heights commanding London. But a German army hidden under English ground! It was a thought to chill the heart.

And it seemed from that wonder of the burning tree, that the enemy mysteriously and terribly present at Midlingham, was present also in Meirion. Lewis, thinking of the country as he knew it, of its wild and desolate hillsides, its deep woods, its wastes and solitary places, could not but confess that no more fit region could be found for the deadly enterprise of secret men. Yet, he thought again, there was but little harm to be done in Meirion to the armies of England or to their munition-ment. They were working for panic terror ? Possibly that might be so ; but the camp under the Highway ? That should be their first object, and no harm had been done there.

Lewis did not know that since the panic

of the horses men had died terribly in that camp ; that it was now a fortified place, with a deep, broad trench, a thick tangle of savage barbed wire about it, and a machine-gun planted at each corner.

# CHAPTER VIII

MR. MERRITT began to pick up his health and spirits a good deal. For the first morning or two of his stay at the doctor's he contented himself with a very comfortable deck chair close to the house, where he sat under the shade of an old mulberry tree beside his wife and watched the bright sunshine on the green lawns, on the creamy crests of the waves, on the headlands of that glorious coast, purple even from afar with the imperial glow of the heather, on the white farmhouses gleaming in the sunlight, high over the sea, far from any turmoil, from any troubling of men.

The sun was hot, but the wind breathed all the while gently, incessantly, from the east, and Merritt, who had come to this quiet place, not only from dismay, but from the stifling and oily airs of the smoky Midland town, said that that east wind, pure and clear and like well water from the rock, was new life to him. He ate a capital dinner at the end of his first day at Porth and took rosy views. As to what they had been talking about the night before, he said to Lewis, no doubt there must be trouble of some sort, and perhaps bad trouble ; still, Kitchener would soon put it all right.

So things went on very well.   Merritt began to stroll about the garden, which was full of the comfortable spaces, groves, and surprises that only country gardens know. To the right of one of the terraces he found an arbour or summer-house covered with white roses, and he was as pleased as if he had discovered the Pole.   He spent a whole day there, smoking and lounging and reading a rubbishy sensational story, and declared that the Devonshire roses had taken many years off his age.   Then on the other side of the garden there was a filbert grove that he had never explored on any of his former visits ; and again there was a find. Deep in the shadow of the filberts was a bubbling well, issuing from rocks, and all manner of green, dewy ferns growing about it and above it, and an angelica springing beside it.   Merritt knelt on his knees, and hollowed his hand and drank the well water. He said (over his port) that night that if all water were like the water of the filbert well the world would turn to teetotalism. It takes a townsman to relish the manifold and exquisite joys of the country.

It was not till he began to venture abroad

that Merritt found that something was lacking of the old rich peace that used to dwell in Meirion. He had a favourite walk which he never neglected, year after year. This walk led along the cliffs towards Meiros, and then one could turn inland and return to Porth by deep winding lanes that went over the Allt. So Merritt set out early one morning and got as far as a sentry-box at the foot of the path that led up to the cliff. There was a sentry pacing up and down in front of the box, and he called on Merritt to produce his pass, or to turn back to the main road. Merritt was a good deal put out, and asked the doctor about this strict guard. And the doctor was surprised.

" I didn't know they had put their bar up there," he said. " I suppose it's wise. We are certainly in the far West here ; still, the Germans might slip round and raid us and do a lot of damage just because Meirion is the last place we should expect them to go for."

" But there are no fortifications, surely, on the cliff ? "

" Oh, no ; I never heard of anything of the kind there."

" Well, what's the point of forbidding the public to go on the cliff, then ? I can

quite understand putting a sentry on the top
to keep a look-out for the enemy.   What I
don't understand is a sentry at the bottom
who can't keep a look-out for anything, as
he can't see the sea.   And why warn the
public off the cliffs ?   I couldn't facilitate a
German landing by standing on Pengareg,
even if I wanted to."

"It is curious," the doctor agreed.
"Some military reasons, I suppose."

He let the matter drop, perhaps because
the matter did not affect him.   People who
live in the country all the year round,
country doctors certainly, are little given
to desultory walking in search of the
picturesque.

Lewis had no suspicion that sentries
whose object was equally obscure were being
dotted all over the country.   There was a
sentry, for example, by the quarry at
Llanfihangel, where the dead woman and
the dead sheep had been found some weeks
before.   The path by the quarry was used
a good deal, and its closing would have
inconvenienced the people of the neighbourhood very considerably.   But the sentry
had his box by the side of the track and had
his orders to keep everybody strictly to the
path, as if the quarry were a secret fort.

It was not known till a month or two ago that one of these sentries was himself a victim of the terror. The men on duty at this place were given certain very strict orders, which from the nature of the case, must have seemed to them unreasonable. For old soldiers, orders are orders ; but here was a young bank clerk, scarcely in training for a couple of months, who had not begun to appreciate the necessity of hard, literal obedience to an order which seemed to him meaningless. He found himself on a remote and lonely hillside, he had not the faintest notion that his every movement was watched ; and he disobeyed a certain instruction that had been given him. The post was found deserted by the relief ; the sentry's dead body was found at the bottom of the quarry.

This by the way ; but Mr. Merritt discovered again and again that things happened to hamper his walks and his wanderings. Two or three miles from Porth there is a great marsh made by the Afon river before it falls into the sea, and here Merritt had been accustomed to botanize mildly. He had learnt pretty accurately the causeways of solid ground that lead through the sea of swamp and ooze and soft yielding soil, and he set out one hot afternoon determined to make a thorough exploration of the marsh, and this time to find that rare Bog Bean, that he felt sure, must grow somewhere in its wide extent.

He got into the by-road that skirts the marsh, and to the gate which he had always used for entrance.

There was the scene as he had known it always, the rich growth of reeds and flags and rushes, the mild black cattle grazing on the " islands " of firm turf, the scented procession of the meadowsweet, the royal glory of the loosestrife, flaming pennons, crimson and golden, of the giant dock.

But they were bringing out a dead man's body through the gate.

A labouring man was holding open the gate on the marsh. Merritt, horrified, spoke to him and asked who it was, and how it had happened.

" They do say he was a visitor at Porth. Somehow he has been drowned in the marsh, whatever."

" But it's perfectly safe. I've been all over it a dozen times."

" Well, indeed, we did always think so. If you did slip by accident, like, and fall into the water, it was not so deep; it was easy enough to climb out again. And this gentleman was quite young, to look at him, poor man; and he has come to Meirion for his pleasure and holiday and found his death in it!"

"Did he do it on purpose? Is it suicide?"

"They say he had no reasons to do that."

Here the sergeant of police in charge of the party interposed, according to orders, which he himself did not understand.

"A terrible thing, sir, to be sure, and a sad pity; and I am sure this is not the sort of sight you have come to see down in Meirion this beautiful summer. So don't you think, sir, that it would be more pleasant like, if you would leave us to this sad business of ours? I have heard many gentlemen staying in Porth say that there is nothing to beat the view from the hill over there, not in the whole of Wales."

Everyone is polite in Meirion, but somehow Merritt understood that, in English, this speech meant "move on."

Merritt moved back to Porth—he was not in the humour for any idle, pleasurable strolling after so dreadful a meeting with

G

death. He made some inquiries in the
town about the dead man, but nothing
seemed known of him. It was said that he
had been on his honeymoon, that he had
been staying at the Porth Castle Hotel ; but
the people of the hotel declared that they
had never heard of such a person. Merritt
got the local paper at the end of the week ;
there was not a word in it of any fatal
accident in the marsh. He met the sergeant of police in the street. That officer
touched his helmet with the utmost polite-
ness and a " hope you are enjoying yourself,
sir ; indeed you do look a lot better
already ; " but as to the poor man who
was found drowned or stifled in the marsh,
he knew nothing.

The next day Merritt made up his mind
to go to the marsh to see whether he could
find anything to account for so strange
a death. What he found was a man with an
armlet standing by the gate. The armlet
had the letters " C. W." on it, which are
understood to mean Coast Watcher. The
Watcher said he had strict instructions to
keep everybody away from the marsh.
Why ? He didn't know, but some said that
the river was changing its course since the
new railway embankment was built, and

the marsh had become dangerous to people
who didn't know it thoroughly.

" Indeed, sir," he added, " it is part of
my orders not to set foot on the other side
of that gate myself, not for one scrag-end of
a minute."

Merritt glanced over the gate incredulously. The marsh looked as it had always
looked ; there was plenty of sound, hard
ground to walk on ; he could see the track
that he used to follow as firm as ever. He
did not believe in the story of the changing
course of the river, and Lewis said he had
never heard of anything of the kind. But
Merritt had put the question in the middle
of general conversation ; he had not led up
to it from any discussion of the death in
the marsh, and so the doctor was taken
unawares. If he had known of the connexion in Merritt's mind between the alleged
changing of the Afon's course and the
tragical event in the marsh, no doubt he
would have confirmed the official explanation. He was, above all things, anxious to
prevent his sister and her husband from
finding out that the invisible hand of terror
that ruled at Midlingham was ruling also
in Meirion.

Lewis himself had little doubt that the

man who was found dead in the marsh had
been struck down by the secret agency, what
ever it was, that had already accomplished
so much of evil ; but it was a chief part of
the terror that no one knew for certain that
this or that particular event was to be
ascribed to it. People do occasionally fall
over cliffs through their own carelessness,
and as the case of Garcia, the Spanish
sailor, showed, cottagers and their wives and
children are now and then the victims of
savage and purposeless violence. Lewis
had never wandered about the marsh
himself ; but Remnant had pottered round
it and about it, and declared that the man
who met his death there—his name was
never known, in Porth at all events—must
either have committed suicide by deliberately lying prone in the ooze and stifling
himself, or else must have been held down in
it. There were no details available, so it was
clear that the authorities had classified this
death with the others ; still, the man might
have committed suicide, or he might have
had a sudden seizure and fallen in the slimy
water face-downwards. And so on : it was
possible to believe that case A *or* B *or* C
was in the category of ordinary accidents or
ordinary crimes. But it was not possible

to believe that A *and* B *and* C were all in
that category.   And thus it was to the end,
and thus it is now.  We know that the
terror reigned, and how it reigned, but there
were many dreadful events ascribed to its
rule about which there must always be
room for doubt.

For example, there was the case of the
*Mary Ann*, the rowing-boat which came to
grief in so strange a manner, almost under
Merritt's eyes.   In my opinion he was quite
wrong in associating the sorry fate of the
boat and her occupants with a system of
signalling by flashlights which he detected
or thought that he detected, on the afternoon in which the *Mary Ann* was capsized.
I believe his signalling theory to be all
nonsense, in spite of the naturalized German
governess who was lodging with her em-
ployers in the suspected house.   But, on
the other hand, there is no doubt in my own
mind that the boat was overturned and
those in it drowned by the work of the
terror.

# CHAPTER IX

LET it be noted carefully that so far
Merritt had not the slightest suspicion that
the terror of Midlingham was quick over
Meirion. Lewis had watched and shep-
herded him carefully. He had let out no
suspicion of what had happened in Meirion,
and before taking his brother-in-law to
the club he had passed round a hint among
the members. He did not tell all the truth
about Midlingham—and here again is a
point of interest, that as the terror deep-
ened the general public co-operated
voluntarily, and, one would say, almost
subconsciously, with the authorities in
concealing what they knew from one
another—but he gave out a desirable
portion of the truth: that his brother-in-
law was " nervy," not by any means up to
the mark, and that it was therefore desirable
that he should be spared the knowledge
of the intolerable and tragic mysteries
which were being enacted all about them.

" He knows about that poor fellow who
was found in the marsh," said Lewis, " and
he has a kind of vague suspicion that there
is something out of the common about the
case ; but no more than that."

" A clear case of suggested, or rather commanded suicide," said Remnant. " I regard it as a strong confirmation of my theory."

" Perhaps so," said the doctor, dreading lest he might have to hear about the Z Ray all over again. " But please don't let anything out to him ; I want him to get built up thoroughly before he goes back to Midlingham."

Then, on the other hand, Merritt was as still as death about the doings of the Midlands ; he hated to think of them, much more to speak of them ; and thus, as I say, he and the men at the Porth Club kept their secrets from one another ; and thus, from the beginning to the end of the terror, the links were not drawn together. In many cases, no doubt, A and B met every day and talked familiarly, it may be confidentially, on other matters of all sorts, each having in his possession half of the truth, which he concealed from the other. So the two halves were never put together to make a whole.

Merritt, as the doctor guessed, had a kind of uneasy feeling — it scarcely amounted to a suspicion—as to the business of the marsh ; chiefly because he thought the official talk about the railway embankment and the course of the river rank nonsense. But finding that nothing more happened, he let the matter drop from his mind, and settled himself down to enjoy his holiday.

He found to his delight that there were no sentries or watchers to hinder him from the approach to Larnac Bay, a delicious cove, a place where the ashgrove and the green meadow and the glistening bracken sloped gently down to red rocks and firm yellow sands. Merritt remembered a rock that formed a comfortable seat, and here he established himself of a golden afternoon, and gazed at the blue of the sea and the crimson bastions and bays of the coast as it bent inward to Sarnau and swept out again southward to the odd-shaped promontory called the Dragon's Head. Merritt gazed on, amused by the antics of the porpoises who were tumbling and splashing and gambolling a little way out at sea, charmed by the pure and radiant air that was so different from the oily smoke that often stood for heaven at Midlingham, and charmed, too, by the white farmhouses dotted here and there on the heights of the curving coast.

Then he noticed a little row-boat at about two hundred yards from the shore. There were two or three people aboard, he could not quite make out how many, and they seemed to be doing something with a line; they were no doubt fishing, and Merritt (who disliked fish) wondered how people could spoil such an afternoon, such a sea, such pellucid and radiant air by trying to catch white, flabby, offensive, evil-smelling creatures that would be excessively nasty when cooked. He puzzled over this problem and turned away from it to the contemplation of the crimson headlands. And then he says that he noticed that signalling was going on. Flashing lights of intense brilliance, he declares, were coming from one of those farms on the heights of the coast; it was as if white fire was spouting from it. Merritt was certain, as the light appeared and disappeared, that some message was being sent, and he regretted that he knew nothing of heliography. Three short flashes, a long and very brilliant flash, then two short flashes. Merritt fumbled in his pocket for pencil and paper so that he might record these signals, and, bringing his eyes down to the sea level, he became aware, with amazement and horror, that the boat had disappeared. All that he could see was some vague, dark object far to westward, running out with the tide.

Now it is certain, unfortunately, that the *Mary Ann* was capsized and that two schoolboys and the sailor in charge were drowned. The bones of the boat were found amongst the rocks far along the coast, and the three bodies were also washed ashore. The sailor could not swim at all, the boys only a little, and it needs an exceptionally fine swimmer to fight against the outward suck of the tide as it rushes past Pengareg Point.

But I have no belief whatever in Merritt's theory. He held (and still holds, for all I know), that the flashes of light which he saw coming from Penyrhaul, the farmhouse on the height, had some connexion with the disaster to the *Mary Ann*. When it was ascertained that a family were spending their summer at the farm, and that the governess was a German, though a long naturalized German, Merritt could not see that there was anything left to argue about, though there might be many details to discover. But, in my opinion, all this was a mere mare's nest ; the flashes of brilliant light were caused, no doubt, by the sun lighting up one window of the farmhouse after the other.

Still, Merritt was convinced from the very first, even before the damning circumstance of the German governess was brought to light ; and on the evening of the disaster, as Lewis and he sat together after dinner, he was endeavouring to put what he called the common sense of the matter to the doctor.

" If you hear a shot," said Merritt, " and you see a man fall, you know pretty well what killed him."

There was a flutter of wild wings in the room. A great moth beat to and fro and dashed itself madly against the ceiling, the walls, the glass bookcase. Then a sputtering sound, a momentary dimming of the lamp. The moth had succeeded in its mysterious quest.

" Can you tell me," said Lewis as if he were answering Merritt, " why moths rush into the flame ? "

Lewis had put his question as to the strange habits of the common moth to Merritt with the deliberate intent of closing the debate on death by heliograph. The query was suggested, of course, by the incident of the moth in the lamp, and Lewis thought that he had said, " Oh, shut up ! " in a somewhat elegant manner. And, in fact Merritt looked dignified, remained silent, and helped himself to port.

That was the end that the doctor had desired. He had no doubt in his own mind that the affair of the *Mary Ann* was but one more item in the long account of horrors that grew larger almost with every day ; and he was in no humour to listen to wild and futile theories as to the manner in which the disaster had been accomplished. Here was a proof that the terror that was upon them was mighty not only on the land but on the waters ; for Lewis could not see that the boat could have been attacked by any ordinary means of destruction. From Merritt's story, it must have been in shallow water. The shore of Larnac Bay shelves very gradually, and the Admiralty charts showed the depth of water two hundred yards out to be only two fathoms ; this would be too shallow for a submarine. And it could not have been shelled, and it could not have been torpedoed ; there was no explosion. The disaster might have been due to carelessness ; boys, he con- sidered, will play the fool anywhere, even

in a boat ; but he did not think so ; the
sailor would have stopped them. And, it
may be mentioned, that the two boys were
as a matter of fact extremely steady,
sensible young fellows, not in the least
likely to play foolish tricks of any kind.

Lewis was immersed in these reflections,
having successfully silenced his brother-in-
law ; he was trying in vain to find some
clue to the horrible enigma. The Midlingham theory of a concealed German force,
hiding in places under the earth, was
extravagant enough, and yet it seemed the
only solution that approached plausibility ;
but then again even a subterranean German
host would hardly account for this wreck-
age of a boat, floating on a calm sea. And
then what of the tree with the burning in
it that had appeared in the garden there a
few weeks ago, and the cloud with a burning
in it that had shown over the trees of the
Midland village ?

I think I have already written something
of the probable emotions of the mathematician confronted suddenly with an
undoubted two-sided triangle. I said, if I
remember, that he would be forced, in
decency, to go mad ; and I believe that
Lewis was very near to this point. He felt

himself confronted with an intolerable
problem that most instantly demanded
solution, and yet, with the same breath, as
it were, denied the possibility of there being
any solution.  People were being killed in
an inscrutable manner by some inscrutable
means, day after day, and one asked
" why " and " how " ;  and there seemed
no answer.  In the Midlands, where every
kind of munitionment was manufactured,
the explanation of German agency was
plausible ;  and even if the subterranean
notion was to be rejected as savouring
altogether too much of the fairy-tale, or
rather of the sensational romance, yet it
was possible that the backbone of the theory
was true ;  the Germans might have planted
their agents in some way or another in the
midst of our factories.  But here in Meirion,
what serious effect could be produced by the
casual and indiscriminate slaughter of a
couple of schoolboys in a boat, of a harmless
holiday-maker in a marsh ?  The creation
of an atmosphere of terror and dismay ?
It was possible, of course, but it hardly
seemed tolerable, in spite of the enormities
of Louvain and of the *Lusitania*.

Into these meditations, and into the still
dignified silence of Merritt broke the rap

on the door of Lewis's man, and those words
which harrass the ease of the country
doctor when he tries to take any ease :
" You're wanted in the surgery, if you
please, sir." Lewis bustled out, and appeared no more that night.

The doctor had been summoned to a little
hamlet on the outskirts of Porth, separated
from it by half a mile or three-quarters of
road. One dignifies, indeed, this settlement
without a name in calling it a hamlet ;
it was a mere row of four cottages, built
about a hundred years ago for the accom-
modation of the workers in a quarry long
since disused. In one of these cottages the
doctor found a father and mother weeping
and crying out to " doctor bach, doctor
bach," and two frightened children, and one
little body, still and dead. It was the
youngest of the three, little Johnny, and he
was dead.

The doctor found that the child had been
asphyxiated. He felt the clothes ; they
were dry ; it was not a case of drowning.
He looked at the neck ; there was no
mark of strangling. He asked the father
how it had happened, and father and
mother, weeping most lamentably, declared

they had no knowledge of how their child had been killed : " unless it was the People that had done it." The Celtic fairies are still malignant. Lewis asked what had happened that evening ; where had the child been ?

" Was he with his brother and sister ? Don't they know anything about it ? "

Reduced into some sort of order from its original piteous confusion, this is the story that the doctor gathered.

All three children had been well and happy through the day. They had walked in with the mother, Mrs. Roberts, to Porth on a marketing expedition in the afternoon ; they had returned to the cottage, had had their tea, and afterwards played about on the road in front of the house. John Roberts had come home somewhat late from his work, and it was after dusk when the family sat down to supper. Supper over, the three children went out again to play with other children from the cottage next door, Mrs. Roberts telling them that they might have half an hour before going to bed.

The two mothers came to the cottage gates at the same moment and called out to their children to come along and be quick

about it.    The two small families had been
playing on the strip of turf across the road,
just by the stile into the fields.    The
children ran across the road ;  all of them
except Johnnie Roberts. His brother Willie
said that just as their mother called them
he heard Johnnie cry out :

   " Oh,  what  is  that beautiful shiny thing
over the stile ? "

# CHAPTER X

THE little Roberts's ran across the road, up the path, and into the lighted room. Then they noticed that Johnnie had not followed them. Mrs. Roberts was doing something in the back kitchen, and Mr. Roberts had gone out to the shed to bring in some sticks for the next morning's fire. Mrs. Roberts heard the children run in and went on with her work. The children whispered to one another that Johnnie would " catch it " when their mother came out of the back room and found him missing ; but they expected he would run in through the open door any minute. But six or seven, perhaps ten, minutes passed, and there was no Johnnie. Then the father and mother came into the kitchen together, and saw that their little boy was not there.

They thought it was some small piece of mischief—that the two other children had hidden the boy somewhere in the room : in the big cupboard perhaps.

" What have you done with him then ? " said Mrs. Roberts. " Come out, you little rascal, directly in a minute."

There was no little rascal to come out,

and Margaret Roberts, the girl, said that
Johnnie had not come across the road with
them : he must be still playing all by
himself by the hedge.

" What did you let him stay like
that for ? " said Mrs. Roberts. " Can't I
trust you for two minutes together ? Indeed to goodness, you are all of you more
trouble than you are worth." She went
to the open door :

" Johnnie ! Come you in directly, or
you will be sorry for it. Johnnie ! "

The poor woman called at the door.
She went out to the gate and called there :

" Come you, little Johnnie. Come you,
bachgen, there's a good boy. I do see you
hiding there."

She thought he must be hiding in the
shadow of the hedge, and that he would
come running and laughing—" he was
always such a happy little fellow "—to her
across the road. But no little merry figure
danced out of the gloom of the still, dark
night ; it was all silence.

It was then, as the mother's heart began
to chill, though she still called cheerfully to
the missing child, that the elder boy told
how Johnnie had said there was something
beautiful by the stile : " and perhaps he did

climb over, and he is running now about the meadow, and has lost his way."

The father got his lantern then, and the whole family went crying and calling about the meadow, promising cakes and sweets and a fine toy to poor Johnnie if he would come to them.

They found the little body, under the ashgrove in the middle of the field. He was quite still and dead, so still that a great moth had settled on his forehead, fluttering away when they lifted him up.

Dr. Lewis heard this story. There was nothing to be done ; little to be said to these most unhappy people.

" Take care of the two that you have left to you," said the doctor as he went away. " Don't let them out of your sight if you can help it. It is dreadful times that we are living in."

It is curious to record that all through these dreadful times the simple little " season " went through its accustomed course at Porth. The war and its consequences had somewhat thinned the numbers of the summer visitors ; still a very fair contingent of them occupied the hotels and boarding-houses and lodging-houses and bathed from the old-fashioned machines

on one beach, or from the new-fashioned
tents on the other, and sauntered in the
sun, or lay stretched out in the shade under
the trees that grow down almost to the
water's edge. Porth never tolerated
Ethiopians or shows of any kind on its
sands, but " The Rockets " did very well
during that summer in their garden enter-
tainment, given in the castle grounds, and
the fit-up companies that came to the
Assembly Rooms are said to have paid their
bills to a woman and to a man.

Porth depends very largely on its midland
and northern custom, custom of a pros-
perous, well-established sort. People who
think Llandudno overcrowded and Colwyn
Bay too raw and red and new, come year
after year to the placid old town in the
south-west and delight in its peace ; and
as I say, they enjoyed themselves much as
usual there in the summer of 1915. Now
and then they became conscious, as Mr.
Merritt became conscious, that they could
not wander about quite in the old way ;
but they accepted sentries and coast-
watchers and people who politely pointed
out the advantages of seeing the view from
this point rather than from that as very
necessary consequences of the dreadful

war that was being waged ; nay, as a
Manchester man said, after having been
turned back from his favourite walk to
Castell Coch, it was gratifying to think that
they were so well looked after.

" So far as I can see," he added, " there's
nothing to prevent a submarine from standing out there by Ynys Sant and landing half
a dozen men in a collapsible boat in any of
these little coves. And pretty fools we
should look, shouldn't we, with our throats
cut on the sands ; or carried back to
Germany in the submarine ? " He found
the coast-watcher half-a-crown.

" That's right, lad," he said, " you give
us the tip."

Now here was a strange thing. The
north-countryman had his thoughts on
elusive submarines and German raiders ;
the watcher had simply received instructions
to keep people off the Castell Coch fields,
without reason assigned. And there can
be no doubt that the authorities themselves,
while they marked out the fields as in the
" terror zone," gave their orders in the dark
and were themselves profoundly in the
dark as to the manner of the slaughter that
had been done there ; for if they had understood what had happened, they would have

understood also that their restrictions were useless.

The Manchester man was warned off his walk about ten days after Johnnie Roberts's death. The Watcher had been placed at his post because, the night before, a young farmer had been found by his wife lying in the grass close to the Castle, with no scar on him, nor any mark of violence, but stone dead.

The wife of the dead man, Joseph Cradock, finding her husband lying motionless on the dewy turf, went white and stricken up the path to the village and got two men who bore the body to the farm. Lewis was sent for, and knew at once when he saw the dead man that he had perished in the way that the little Roberts boy had perished— whatever that awful way might be. Cradock had been asphyxiated ; and here again there was no mark of a grip on the throat. It might have been a piece of work by Burke and Hare, the doctor reflected ; a pitch plaster might have been clapped over the man's mouth and nostrils and held there.

Then a thought struck him ; his brother-in-law had talked of a new kind of poison gas that was said to be used against the munition workers in the Midlands : was it possible that the deaths of the man and the boy were due to some such instrument ? He applied his tests but could find no trace of any gas having been employed. Carbonic acid gas ? A man could not be killed with that in the open air ; to be fatal that required a confined space, such a position as the bottom of a huge vat or of a well.

He did not know how Cradock had been killed ; he confessed it to himself. He had been suffocated ; that was all he could say.

It seemed that the man had gone out at about half-past nine to look after some beasts. The field in which they were was about five minutes walk from the house. He told his wife he would be back in a quarter of an hour or twenty minutes. He did not return, and when he had been gone for three-quarters of an hour Mrs. Cradock went out to look for him. She went into the field where the beasts were, and everything seemed all right, but there was no trace of Cradock. She called out ; there was no answer.

Now the meadow in which the cattle were pastured is high ground ; a hedge divides it from the fields which fall gently down to the castle and the sea. Mrs. Cradock hardly seemed able to say why, having failed to find her husband among his beasts, she turned to the path which led to Castell Coch. She said at first that she had thought that one of the oxen might have broken through the hedge and strayed, and that Cradock had perhaps gone after it. And then, correcting herself, she said :

" There was that ; and then there was something else that I could not make out at all. It seemed to me that the hedge did look different from usual. To be sure, things do look different at night, and there was a bit of seamist about, but somehow it did look odd to me, and I said to myself, ' have I lost my way, then ? ' "

She declared that the shape of the trees in the hedge appeared to have changed, and besides, it had a look " as if it was lighted up, somehow," and so she went on towards the stile to see what all this could be, and when she came near everything was as usual. She looked over the stile and called and hoped to see her husband coming towards her or to hear his voice ; but there was no answer, and glancing down the path she saw, or thought she saw, some sort of brightness on the ground, " a dim sort of light like a bunch of glow-worms in a hedge-bank.

" And so I climbed over the stile and went down the path, and the light seemed to melt away ; and there was my poor husband lying on his back, saying not a word to me when I spoke to him and touched him."

So for Lewis the terror blackened and became altogether intolerable, and others, he perceived, felt as he did. He did not know, he never asked whether the men at the club had heard of these deaths of the child and the young farmer ; but no one spoke of them. Indeed, the change was evident ; at the beginning of the terror men spoke of nothing else ; now it had become all too awful for ingenious chatter or laboured and grotesque theories. And Lewis had received a letter from his brother-in-law at Midlingham ; it contained the sentence, " I am afraid Fanny's health has not greatly benefited by her visit to Porth ; there are still several symptoms I don't at all like." And this told him, in a phraseology that the doctor and Merritt had agreed upon, that the terror remained heavy in the Midland town.

It was soon after the death of Cradock that people began to tell strange tales of a sound that was to be heard of nights about the hills and valleys to the northward of Porth. A man who had missed the last train from Meiros and had been forced to tramp the ten miles between Meiros and Porth seems to have been the first to hear it. He said he had got to the top of the hill by Tredonoc, somewhere between half-past ten and eleven, when he first noticed an odd noise that he could not make out at all ; it was like a shout, a long, drawn-out, dismal wail coming from a great way off, faint with distance. He stopped to listen, thinking at first that it might be owls hooting in the woods ; but it was different he said, from that : it was a long cry, and then there was silence and then it began over again. He could make nothing of it, and feeling frightened, he did not quite know of what, he walked on briskly and was glad to see the lights of Porth station.

He told his wife of this dismal sound that night, and she told the neighbours, and most of them thought that it was "all fancy"—or drink, or the owls after all. But the night after, two or three people, who had been to some small merrymaking in a cottage just off the Meiros road, heard the sound as they were going home, soon after ten. They, too, described it as a long, wailing cry, indescribably dismal in the stillness of the autumn night; "like the ghost of a voice," said one; "as if it came up from the bottom of the earth," said another.

# CHAPTER XI

LET it be remembered, again and again, that, all the while that the terror lasted, there was no common stock of information as to the dreadful things that were being done. The press had not said one word upon it, there was no criterion by which the mass of the people could separate fact from mere vague rumour, no test by which ordinary misadventure or disaster could be distinguished from the achievements of the secret and awful force that was at work.

And so with every event of the passing day. A harmless commercial traveller might show himself in the course of his business in the tumbledown main street of Meiros and find himself regarded with looks of fear and suspicion as a possible worker of murder, while it is likely enough that the true agents of the terror went quite unnoticed. And since the real nature of all this mystery of death was unknown, it followed easily that the signs and warnings and omens of it were all the more unknown. Here was horror, there was horror; but there was no links to join one horror with another; no common basis of knowledge from which the connexion between this horror and that horror might be inferred.

So there was no one who suspected at all that this dismal and hollow sound that was now heard of nights in the region to the north of Porth, had any relation at all to the case of the little girl who went out one afternoon to pick purple flowers and never returned, or to the case of the man whose body was taken out of the peaty slime of the marsh, or to the case of Cradock, dead in his fields, with a strange glimmering of light about his body, as his wife reported. And it is a question as to how far the rumour of this melancholy, nocturnal summons got abroad at all. Lewis heard of it, as a country doctor hears of most things, driving up and down the lanes, but he heard of it without much interest, with no sense that it was in any sort of relation to the terror. Remnant had been given the story of the hollow and echoing voice of the darkness in a coloured and picturesque form ; he employed a Tredonoc man to work in his garden once a week. The gardener had not heard the summons himself, but he knew a man who had done so.

" Thomas Jenkins, Pentoppin, he did

put his head out late last night to see what the weather was like, as he was cutting a field of corn the next day, and he did tell me that when he was with the Methodists in Cardigan he did never hear no singing eloquence in the chapels that was like to it. He did declare it was like a wailing of Judgment Day.''

Remnant considered the matter, and was inclined to think that the sound must be caused by a subterranean inlet of the sea ; there might be, he supposed, an imperfect or half-opened or tortuous blow-hole in the Tredonoc woods, and the noise of the tide, surging up below, might very well produce that effect of a hollow wailing, far away. But neither he nor any one else paid much attention to the matter ; save the few who heard the call at dead of night, as it echoed awfully over the black hills.

The sound had been heard for three or perhaps four nights, when the people coming out of Tredonoc church afte morning service on Sunday noticed that there was a big yellow sheepdog in the churchyard. The dog, it appeared, had been waiting for the congregation ; for it at once attached itself to them, at first to the whole body, and then to a group of half a dozen who took the turning to the right. Two of these presently went off over the fields to their respective houses, and four strolled on in the leisurely Sunday-morning manner of the country, and these the dog followed, keeping to heel all the time. The men were talking hay, corn and markets and paid no attention to the animal, and so they strolled along the autumn lane till they came to a gate in the hedge, whence a roughly made farm road went through the fields, and dipped down into the woods and to Treff Loyne farm.

Then the dog became like a possessed creature. He barked furiously. He ran up to one of the men and looked up at him, " as if he were begging for his life," as the man said, and then rushed to the gate and stood by it, wagging his tail and barking at intervals. The men stared and laughed.

" Whose dog will that be ? " said one of them.

" It will be Thomas Griffith's, Treff Loyne," said another.

" Well, then, why doesn't he go home ? Go home, then ! " He went through the gesture of picking up a stone from the road and throwing it at the dog. "Go home, then! Over the gate with you."

But the dog never stirred. He barked and whined and ran up to the men and then back to the gate. At last he came to one of them, and crawled and abased himself on the ground and then took hold of the man's coat and tried to pull him in the direction of the gate. The farmer shook the dog off, and the four went on their way; and the dog stood in the road and watched them and then put up its head and uttered a long and dismal howl that was despair.

The four farmers thought nothing of it; sheepdogs in the country are dogs to look after sheep, and their whims and fancies are not studied. But the yellow dog—he was a kind of degenerate colley—haunted the Tredonoc lanes from that day. He came to a cottage door one night and scratched at it, and when it was opened lay down, and then, barking, ran to the garden gate and waited, entreating, as it seemed, the cottager to follow him. They drove him away and again he gave that long howl of anguish. It was almost as bad, they said, as the noise that they had heard a few nights before. And then it occurred to somebody,

I

so far as I can make out with no particular
reference to the odd conduct of the Treff
Loyne sheepdog, that Thomas Griffith had
not been seen for some time past.  He had
missed market day at Porth, he had not
been at Tredonoc church, where he was a
pretty regular attendant on Sunday ; and
then, as heads were put together, it appeared
that nobody had seen any of the Griffith
family for days and days.

Now in a town, even in a small town, this
process of putting heads together is a pretty
quick business.  In the country, especially
in a countryside of wild lands and scattered
and lonely farms and cottages, the affair
takes time.  Harvest was going on, everybody was busy in his own fields, and after
the long day's hard work neither the
farmer nor his men felt inclined to stroll
about in search of news or gossip.  A
harvester at the day's end is ready for
supper and sleep and for nothing else.

And so it was late in that week when it
was discovered that Thomas Griffith and
all his house had vanished from this world.

I have often been reproached for my
curiosity over questions which are apparently of slight importance, or of no importance at all.  I love to inquire, for instance,

into the question of the visibility of a
lighted candle at a distance. Suppose,
that is, a candle lighted on a still, dark
night in the country; what is the greatest
distance at which you can see that there is a
light at all? And then as to the human
voice; what is its carrying distance, under
good conditions, as a mere sound, apart
from any matter of making out words that
may be uttered?

They are trivial questions, no doubt, but
they have always interested me, and the
latter point has its application to the
strange business of Treff Loyne. That
melancholy and hollow sound, that wailing
summons that appalled the hearts of those
who heard it was, indeed, a human voice,
produced in a very exceptional manner;
and it seems to have been heard at points
varying from a mile and a half to two miles
from the farm. I do not know whether this
is anything extraordinary; I do not know
whether the peculiar method of production
was calculated to increase or to diminish
the carrying power of the sound.

Again and again I have laid emphasis
in this story of the terror on the strange
isolation of many of the farms and cottages
in Meirion. I have done so in the effort

to convince the townsman of something that he has never known. To the Londoner a house a quarter of a mile from the outlying suburban lamp, with no other dwelling within two hundred yards, is a lonely house, a place to fit with ghosts and mysteries and terrors. How can he understand then, the true loneliness of the white farmhouses of Meirion, dotted here and there, for the most part not even on the little lanes and deep winding by-ways, but set in the very heart of the fields, or alone on huge bastioned headlands facing the sea, and whether on the high verge of the sea or on the hills or in the hollows of the inner country, hidden from the sight of men, far from the sound of any common call. There is Penyrhaul, for example, the farm from which the foolish Merritt thought he saw signals of light being made : from seaward it is of course, widely visible ; but from landward, owing partly to the curving and indented configuration of the bay, I doubt whether any other habitation views it from a nearer distance than three miles.

And of all these hidden and remote places, I doubt if any is so deeply buried as Treff Loyne. I have little or no Welsh, I

am sorry to say, but I suppose that the
name is corrupted from Trellwyn, or Tref-y-
llwyn, "the place in the grove," and,
indeed, it lies in the very heart of dark,
overhanging woods. A deep, narrow valley
runs down from the high lands of the Allt,
through these woods, through steep hillsides of bracken and gorse, right down to the
great marsh, whence Merritt saw the dead
man being carried. The valley lies away
from any road, even from that by-road,
little better than a bridlepath, where the
four farmers, returning from church were
perplexed by the strange antics of the sheepdog. One cannot say that the valley is
overlooked, even from a distance, for so
narrow is it that the ashgroves that rim
it on either side seem to meet and shut it in.
I, at all events, have never found any high
place from which Treff Loyne is visible;
though, looking down from the Allt, I have
seen blue wood-smoke rising from its hidden
chimneys.

Such was the place, then, to which one
September afternoon a party went up to
discover what had happened to Griffith
and his family. There were half a dozen
farmers, a couple of policemen, and four
soldiers, carrying their arms; those last

had been lent by the officer commanding at the camp. Lewis, too, was of the party; he had heard by chance that no one knew what had become of Griffith and his family; and he was anxious about a young fellow, a painter, of his acquaintance, who had been lodging at Treff Loyne all the summer.

They all met by the gate of Tredonoc churchyard, and tramped solemnly along the narrow lane; all of them, I think, with some vague discomfort of mind, with a certain shadowy fear, as of men who do not quite know what they may encounter. Lewis heard the corporal and the three soldiers arguing over their orders.

" The Captain says to me," muttered the corporal, "'Don't hesitate to shoot if there's any trouble.' 'Shoot what, sir?' I says. 'The trouble,' says he, and that's all I could get out of him."

The men grumbled in reply; Lewis thought he heard some obscure reference to rat-poison, and wondered what they were talking about.

They came to the gate in the hedge, where the farm road led down to Treff Loyne. They followed this track, roughly made, with grass growing up between its loosely laid stones, down by the hedge

from field to wood, till at last they came to
the sudden walls of the valley, and the
sheltering groves of the ash trees. Here
the way curved down the steep hillside, and
bent southward, and followed henceforward
the hidden hollow of the valley, under the
shadow of the trees.

Here was the farm enclosure ; the outlying walls of the yard, and the barns and
sheds and outhouses. One of the farmers
threw open the gate and walked into the
yard, and forthwith began bellowing at the
top of his voice :

" Thomas Griffith ! Thomas Griffith !
Where be you, Thomas Griffith ? "

The rest followed him. The corporal
snapped out an order over his shoulder, and
there was a rattling metallic noise as the
men fixed their bayonets and became in an
instant dreadful dealers out of death, in place
of harmless fellows with a feeling for beer.

" Thomas Griffith ! " again bellowed the
farmer.

There was no answer to this summons.
But they found poor Griffith lying on his
face at the edge of the pond in the middle
of the yard. There was a ghastly wound
in his side, as if a sharp stake had been
driven into his body.

# CHAPTER XII

Iᴛ was a still September afternoon. No
wind stirred in the hanging woods that
were dark all about the ancient house
of Treff Loyne ; the only sound in the
dim air was the lowing of the cattle ; they
had wandered, it seemed, from the fields and
had come in by the gate of the farmyard and stood there melancholy, as if they
mourned for their dead master. And the
horses ; four great, heavy, patient-looking
beasts they were there too, and in the lower
field the sheep were standing, as if they
waited to be fed.

" You would think they all knew there
was something wrong," one of the soldiers
muttered to another. A pale sun showed
for a moment and glittered on their
bayonets. They were standing about the
body of poor, dead Griffith, with a certain
grimness growing on their faces and harden-
ing there. Their corporal snapped something at them again ; they were quite
ready. Lewis knelt down by the dead man
and looked closely at the great gaping
wound in his side.

" He's been dead a long time," he said.
" A week, two weeks, perhaps. He was

killed by some sharp pointed weapon. How about the family? How many are there of them? I never attended them."

" There was Griffith, and his wife, and his son Thomas and Mary Griffith, his daughter. And I do think there was a gentleman lodging with them this summer."

That was from one of the farmers. They all looked at one another, this party of rescue, who knew nothing of the danger that had smitten this house of quiet people, nothing of the peril which had brought them to this pass of a farmyard with a dead man in it, and his beasts standing patiently about him, as if they waited for the farmer to rise up and give them their food. Then the party turned to the house. It was an old, sixteenth century building, with the singular, round, " Flemish " chimney that is characteristic of Meirion. The walls were snowy with whitewash, the windows were deeply set and stone mullioned, and a solid, stone-tiled porch sheltered the doorway from any winds that might penetrate to the hollow of that hidden valley. The windows were shut tight. There was no sign of any life or movement about the place. The party of men looked at one another, and the churchwarden amongst the farmers, the sergeant of police, Lewis, and the corporal drew together.

"What is it to goodness, doctor?" said the churchwarden.

"I can tell you nothing at all—except that that poor man there has been pierced to the heart," said Lewis.

"Do you think they are inside and they will shoot us?" said another farmer. He had no notion of what he meant by "they," and no one of them knew better than he. They did not know what the danger was, or where it might strike them, or whether it was from without or from within. They stared at the murdered man, and gazed dismally at one another.

"Come!" said Lewis," we must do something. We must get into the house and see what is wrong."

"Yes, but suppose they are at us while we are getting in," said the sergeant. "Where shall we be then, Doctor Lewis?"

The corporal put one of his men by the gate at the top of the farmyard, another at the gate by the bottom of the farmyard, and told them to challenge and shoot. The doctor and the rest opened the little gate of the front garden and went up to the porch and stood listening by the

door. It was all dead silence. Lewis took
an ash stick from one of the farmers and
beat heavily three times on the old, black,
oaken door studded with antique nails.

He struck three thundering blows, and
then they all waited. There was no answer
from within. He beat again, and still
silence. He shouted to the people within,
but there was no answer. They all turned
and looked at one another, that party of
quest and rescue who knew not what
they sought, what enemy they were to
encounter. There was an iron ring on the
door. Lewis turned it but the door stood
fast ; it was evidently barred and bolted.
The sergeant of police called out to open,
but again there was no answer.

They consulted together. There was
nothing for it but to blow the door open, and
some one of them called in a loud voice to
anybody that might be within to stand
away from the door, or they would be
killed. And at this very moment the yellow
sheepdog came bounding up the yard from
the woods and licked their hands and
fawned on them and barked joyfully.

" Indeed now," said one of the farmers,
" he did know that there was something
amiss. A pity it was, Thomas Williams,

that we did not follow him when he implored us last Sunday."

The corporal motioned the rest of the party back, and they stood looking fearfully about them at the entrance to the porch. The corporal disengaged his bayonet and shot into the keyhole, calling out once more before he fired. He shot and shot again ; so heavy and firm was the ancient door, so stout its bolts and fastenings. At last he had to fire at the massive hinges, and then they all pushed together and the door lurched open and fell forward. The corporal raised his left hand and stepped back a few paces. He hailed his two men at the top and bottom of the farmyard. They were all right, they said. And so the party climbed and struggled over the fallen door into the passage, and into the kitchen of the farmhouse.

Young Griffith was lying dead before the hearth, before a dead fire of white wood ashes. They went on towards the "parlour," and in the doorway of the room was the body of the artist, Secretan, as if he had fallen in trying to get to the kitchen. Upstairs the two women, Mrs. Griffiths and her daughter, a girl of eighteen, were lying together on the bed in

the big bedroom, clasped in each others'
arms.

They went about the house, searched
the pantries, the back kitchen and the
cellars ; there was no life in it.

" Look ! " said Dr. Lewis, when they
came back to the big kitchen, " look !
It is as if they had been besieged. Do you
see that piece of bacon, half gnawed
through ? "

Then they found these pieces of bacon,
cut from the sides on the kitchen wall,
here and there about the house. There
was no bread in the place, no milk, no
water.

" And," said one of the farmers, " they
had the best water here in all Meirion.
The well is down there in the wood ; it is
most famous water. The old people did
use to call it Ffynnon Teilo ; it was Saint
Teilo's Well, they did say."

" They must have died of thirst," said
Lewis. " They have been dead for days
and days."

The group of men stood in the big kitchen
and stared at one another, a dreadful
perplexity in their eyes. The dead were all
about them, within the house and without
it ; and it was in vain to ask why they had

died thus.   The old man had been killed with the piercing thrust of some sharp weapon ;  the rest had perished, it seemed probable, of thirst ;  but what possible enemy was this that had besieged the farm and shut in its inhabitants ?   There was no answer.

The sergeant of police spoke of getting a cart and taking the bodies into Porth, and Dr. Lewis went into the parlour that Secretan had used as a sitting-room, intending to gather any possessions or effects of the dead artist that he might find there. Half a dozen portfolios were piled up in one corner, there were some books on a side table, a fishing-rod and basket behind the door—that seemed all.   No doubt there would be clothes and such matters upstairs, and Lewis was about to rejoin the rest of the party in the kitchen, when he looked down at some scattered papers lying with the books on the side table.   On one of the sheets he read to his astonishment the words : "Dr. James Lewis, Porth."   This was written in a staggering trembling scrawl, and examining the other leaves he saw that they were covered with writing.

The table stood in a dark corner of the room, and Lewis gathered up the sheets of

paper and took them to the window-
ledge and began to read, amazed at certain
phrases that had caught his eye. But the
manuscript was in disorder ; as if the dead
man who had written it had not been equal
to the task of gathering the leaves into
their proper sequence ; it was some time
before the doctor had each page in its
place. This was the statement that he
read, with ever-growing wonder, while a
couple of the farmers were harnessing one
of the horses in the yard to a cart, and
the others were bringing down the dead
women.

"I do not think that I can last much
longer. We shared out the last drops of
water a long time ago. I do not know how
many days ago. We fall asleep and dream
and walk about the house in our dreams,
and I am often not sure whether I am awake
or still dreaming, and so the days and nights
are confused in my mind. I awoke not
long ago, at least I suppose I awoke and
found I was lying in the passage. I had a
confused feeling that I had had an awful
dream which seemed horribly real, and I
thought for a moment what a relief it was
to know that it wasn't true, whatever it

might have been. I made up my mind to have a good long walk to freshen myself up, and then I looked round and found that I had been lying on the stones of the passage ; and it all came back to me. There was no walk for me.

"I have not seen Mrs. Griffith or her daughter for a long while. They said they were going upstairs to have a rest. I heard them moving about the room at first, now I can hear nothing. Young Griffith is lying in the kitchen, before the hearth. He was talking to himself about the harvest and the weather when I last went into the kitchen. He didn't seem to know I was there, as he went gabbling on in a low voice very fast, and then he began to call the dog, Tiger.

"There seems no hope for any of us. We are in the dream of death . . . ."

Here the manuscript became unintelligible for half a dozen lines. Secretan had written the words " dream of death " three or four times over. He had begun a fresh word and had scratched it out and then followed strange, unmeaning characters, the script, as Lewis thought, of a terrible language. And then the writing became clear, clearer than it was at the beginning of the manuscript, and the sentences flowed more easily, as if the cloud on Secretan's mind had lifted for a while.  There was a fresh start, as it were, and the writer began again, in ordinary letter-form :

" DEAR LEWIS,

" I hope you will excuse all this confusion and wandering.  I intended to begin a proper letter to you, and now I find all that stuff that you have been reading—if this ever gets into your hands.  I have not the energy even to tear it up.  If you read it you will know to what a sad pass I had come when it was written.  It looks like delirium or a bad dream, and even now, though my mind seems to have cleared up a good deal, I have to hold myself in tightly to be sure that the experiences of the last days in this awful place are true, real things, not a long nightmare from which I shall wake up presently and find myself in my rooms at Chelsea.

" I have said of what I am writing, ' if it ever gets into your hands,' and I am not at all sure that it ever will.  If what is happening here is happening everywhere else, then I suppose, the world is coming to an end.  I cannot understand it, even now

I can hardly believe it. I know that I
dream such wild dreams and walk in such
mad fancies that I have to look out and
look about me to make sure that I am not
still dreaming.

"Do you remember that talk we had
about two months ago when I dined with
you? We got on, somehow or other, to
space and time, and I think we agreed that
as soon as one tried to reason about space
and time one was landed in a maze of
contradictions. You said something to
the effect that it was very curious, but this
was just like a dream. 'A man will sometimes wake himself from his crazy dream,'
you said, 'by realizing that he is thinking
nonsense.' And we both wondered whether
these contradictions that one can't avoid
if one begins to think of time and space may
not really be proofs that the whole of life
is a dream, and the moon and the stars
bits of nightmare. I have often thought
over that lately. I kick at the walls as
Dr. Johnson kicked at the stone, to make
sure that the things about me are there.
And then that other question gets into my
mind—is the world really coming to an end,
the world as we have always known it;
and what on earth will this new world be

like ? I can't imagine it ; it's a story like Noah's Ark and the Flood. People used to talk about the end of the world and fire, but no one ever thought of anything like this.

"And then there's another thing that bothers me. Now and then I wonder whether we are not all mad together in this house. In spite of what I see and know, or, perhaps, I should say, because what I see and know is so impossible, I wonder whether we are not all suffering from a delusion. Perhaps we are our own gaolers, and we are really free to go out and live. Perhaps what we think we see is not there at all. I believe I have heard of whole families going mad together, and I may have come under the influence of the house, having lived in it for the last four months. I know there have been people who have been kept alive by their keepers forcing food down their throats, because they are quite sure that their throats are closed, so that they feel they are unable to swallow a morsel. I wonder now and then whether we are all like this in Treff Loyne ; yet in my heart I feel sure that it is not so.

"Still, I do not want to leave a mad-man's letter behind me, and so I will not

tell you the full story of what I have seen,
or believe I have seen.  If I am a sane man
you will be able to fill in the blanks for
yourself from your own knowledge.  If I
am mad, burn the letter and say nothing
about it.  Or perhaps—and indeed, I am
not quite sure—I may wake up and hear
Mary Griffith calling to me in her cheerful
sing-song that breakfast will be ready
' directly, in a minute,' and I shall enjoy it
and walk over to Porth and tell you the
queerest, most horrible dream that a man
ever had, and ask what I had better take.

" I think that it was on a Tuesday that
we first noticed that there was something
queer about, only at the time we didn't
know that there was anything really queer
in what we noticed.  I had been out since
nine o'clock in the morning trying to
paint the marsh, and I found it a very
tough job.  I came home about five or six
o'clock and found the family at Treff Loyne
laughing at old Tiger, the sheepdog.  He
was making short runs from the farmyard
to the door of the house, barking, with
quick, short yelps.  Mrs. Griffith and Miss
Griffith were standing by the porch, and
the dog would go to them, look in their
faces, and then run up the farmyard to the

gate, and then look back with that eager
yelping bark, as if he were waiting for the
women to follow him. Then, again and
again, he ran up to them and tugged at
their skirts as if he would pull them by
main force away from the house.

" Then the men came home from the fields
and he repeated this performance. The
dog was running all up and down the
farmyard, in and out of the barn and sheds
yelping, barking ; and always with that
eager run to the person he addressed, and
running away directly, and looking back
as if to see whether we were following him.
When the house-door was shut and they
all sat down to supper, he would give them
no peace, till at last they turned him out of
doors. And then he sat in the porch and
scratched at the door with his claws, barking all the while. When the daughter
brought in my meal, she said : ' We can't
think what is come to old Tiger, and indeed,
he has always been a good dog, too.'

" The dog barked and yelped and whined
and scratched at the door all through the
evening. They let him in once, but he
seemed to have become quite frantic. He
ran up to one member of the family after
another ; his eyes were bloodshot and his

mouth was foaming, and he tore at their
clothes till they drove him out again into
the darkness.  Then he broke into a long,
lamentable howl of anguish, and we heard
no more of him."

# CHAPTER XIII

" I SLEPT ill that night. I awoke again and again from uneasy dreams, and I seemed in my sleep to hear strange calls and noises and a sound of murmurs and beatings on the door. There were deep, hollow voices, too, that echoed in my sleep, and when I woke I could hear the autumn wind, mournful, on the hills above us. I started up once with a dreadful scream in my ears ; but then the house was all still, and I fell again into uneasy sleep.

"It was soon after dawn when I finally roused myself. The people in the house were talking to each other in high voices, arguing about something that I did not understand.

"' It is those damned gipsies, I tell you,' said old Griffith.

"' What would they do a thing like that for ? ' asked Mrs. Griffiths. ' If it was stealing now——"

"' It is more likely that John Jenkins has done it out of spite,' said the son. 'He said that he would remember you when we did catch him poaching.'

"They seemed puzzled and angry, so far as I could make out, but not at all frightened.

I got up and began to dress. I don't think
I looked out of the window. The glass on
my dressing-table is high and broad, and
the window is small; one would have to
poke one's head round the glass to see
anything.

"'The voices were still arguing downstairs.
I heard the old man say, ' Well, here's for
a beginning anyhow,' and then the door
slammed.

"A minute later the old man shouted, I
think, to his son. Then there was a great
noise which I will not describe more
particularly, and a dreadful screaming and
crying inside the house and a sound of
rushing feet. They all cried out at once to
each other. I heard the daughter crying,
' it is no good, mother, he is dead, indeed
they have killed him,' and Mrs. Griffith
screaming to the girl to let her go. And
then one of them rushed out of the kitchen
and shot the great bolts of oak across the
door, just as something beat against it with
a thundering crash.

"I ran downstairs. I found them all in
wild confusion, in an agony of grief and
horror and amazement. They were like
people who had seen something so awful
that they had gone mad.

" I went to the window looking out on the farmyard. I won't tell you all that I saw. But I saw poor old Griffith lying by the pond, with the blood pouring out of his side.

" I wanted to go out to him and bring him in. But they told me that he must be stone dead, and such things also that it was quite plain that anyone who went out of the house would not live more than a moment. We could not believe it, even as we gazed at the body of the dead man ; but it was there. I used to wonder sometimes what one would feel like if one saw an apple drop from the tree and shoot up into the air and disappear. I think I know now how one would feel.

" Even then we couldn't believe that it would last. We were not seriously afraid for ourselves. We spoke of getting out in an hour or two, before dinner anyhow. It couldn't last, because it was impossible. Indeed, at twelve o'clock young Griffith said he would go down to the well by the back way and draw another pail of water. I went to the door and stood by it. He had not gone a dozen yards before they were on him. He ran for his life, and we had all we could do to bar the door in time. And then I began to get frightened.

"Still we could not believe in it. Somebody would come along shouting in an hour or two and it would all melt away and vanish. There could not be any real danger. There was plenty of bacon in the house, and half the weekly baking of loaves and some beer in the cellar and a pound or so of tea, and a whole pitcher of water that had been drawn from the well the night before. We could do all right for the day and in the morning it would have all gone away.

"But day followed day and it was still there. I knew Treff Loyne was a lonely place—that was why I had gone there, to have a long rest from all the jangle and rattle and turmoil of London, that makes a man alive and kills him too. I went to Treff Loyne because it was buried in the narrow valley under the ash trees, far away from any track. There was not so much as a footpath that was near it ; no one ever came that way. Young Griffith had told me that it was a mile and a half to the nearest house, and the thought of the silent peace and retirement of the farm used to be a delight to me.

" And now this thought came back without delight, with terror. Griffith thought that a shout might be heard on a still night up away on the Allt, ' if a man was listening for it,' he added, doubtfully. My voice was clearer and stronger than his, and on the second night I said I would go up to my bedroom and call for help through the open window. I waited till it was all dark and still, and looked out through the window before opening it. And then I saw over the ridge of the long barn across the yard what looked like a tree, though I knew there was no tree there. It was a dark mass against the sky, with wide-spread boughs, a tree of thick, dense growth. I wondered what this could be, and I threw open the window, not only because I was going to call for help, but because I wanted to see more clearly what the dark growth over the barn really was.

" I saw in the depth of the dark of it points of fire, and colours in light, all glowing and moving, and the air trembled. I stared out into the night, and the dark tree lifted over the roof of the barn and rose up in the air and floated towards me. I did not move till at the last moment when it was close to the house ; and then

I saw what it was and banged the window down only just in time. I had to fight, and I saw the tree that was like a burning cloud rise up in the night and sink again and settle over the barn.

"I told them downstairs of this. They sat with white faces, and Mrs. Griffith said that ancient devils were let loose and had come out of the trees and out of the old hills because of the wickedness that was on the earth. She began to murmur something to herself, something that sounded to me like broken-down Latin.

"I went up to my room again an hour later, but the dark tree swelled over the barn. Another day went by, and at dusk I looked out, but the eyes of fire were watching me. I dared not open the window.

"And then I thought of another plan. There was the great old fireplace, with the round Flemish chimney going high above the house. If I stood beneath it and shouted I thought perhaps the sound might be carried better than if I called out of the window; for all I knew the round chimney might act as a sort of megaphone. Night after night, then, I stood in the hearth and called for help from nine o'clock to eleven.

I thought of the lonely place, deep in the valley of the ashtrees, of the lonely hills and lands about it. I thought of the little cottages far away and hoped that my voice might reach to those within them. I thought of the winding lane high on the Allt, and of the few men that came there of nights ; but I hoped that my cry might come to one of them.

" But we had drunk up the beer, and we would only let ourselves have water by little drops, and on the fourth night my throat was dry, and I began to feel strange and weak ; I knew that all the voice I had in my lungs would hardly reach the length of the field by the farm.

" It was then we began to dream of wells and fountains, and water coming very cold, in little drops, out of rocky places in the middle of a cool wood. We had given up all meals ; now and then one would cut a lump from the sides of bacon on the kitchen wall and chew a bit of it, but the saltness was like fire.

" There was a great shower of rain one night. The girl said we might open a window and hold out bowls and basins and catch the rain. I spoke of the cloud with burning eyes. She said ' we will go to the window in the dairy at the back, and one of us can get some water at all events.' She stood up with her basin on the stone slab in the dairy and looked out and heard the plashing of the rain, falling very fast. And she unfastened the catch of the window and had just opened it gently with one hand, for about an inch, and had her basin in the other hand. 'And then,' said she, 'there was something that began to tremble and shudder and shake as it did when we went to the Choral Festival at St. Teilo's, and the organ played, and there was the cloud and the burning close before me.'

"And then we began to dream, as I say. I woke up in my sitting-room one hot afternoon when the sun was shining, and I had been looking and searching in my dream all through the house, and I had gone down to the old cellar that wasn't used, the cellar with the pillars and the vaulted roof, with an iron pike in my hand. Something said to me that there was water there, and in my dream I went to a heavy stone by the middle pillar and raised it up, and there beneath was a bubbling well of cold, clear water, and I had just hollowed my hand to drink it when I woke. I went into the kitchen and told young Griffith.

I said I was sure there was water there.
He shook his head, but he took up the great
kitchen poker and we went down to the
old cellar. I showed him the stone by
the pillar, and he raised it up. But there
was no well.

"Do you know, I reminded myself of
many people whom I have met in life?
I would not be convinced. I was sure that,
after all, there was a well there. They had
a butcher's cleaver in the kitchen and I
took it down to the old cellar and hacked
at the ground with it. The others didn't
interfere with me. We were getting past
that. We hardly ever spoke to one another.
Each one would be wandering about the
house, upstairs and downstairs, each one
of us, I suppose, bent on his own foolish
plan and mad design, but we hardly ever
spoke. Years ago, I was an actor for a bit,
and I remember how it was on first nights;
the actors treading softly up and down the
wings, by their entrance, their lips moving
and muttering over the words of their parts,
but without a word for one another. So
it was with us. I came upon young
Griffith one evening evidently trying to
make a subterranean passage under one
of the walls of the house. I knew he was

mad, as he knew I was mad when he saw
me digging for a well in the cellar; but
neither said anything to the other.

"Now we are past all this. We are too
weak. We dream when we are awake and
when we dream we think we wake. Night
and day come and go and we mistake one
for another; I hear Griffith murmuring
to himself about the stars when the sun is
high at noonday, and at midnight I have
found myself thinking that I walked in
bright sunlit meadows beside cold, rushing
streams that flowed from high rocks.

"Then at the dawn figures in black robes,
carrying lighted tapers in their hands pass
slowly about and about; and I hear great
rolling organ music that sounds as if some
tremendous rite were to begin, and voices
crying in an ancient song shrill from the
depths of the earth.

"Only a little while ago I heard a voice
which sounded as if it were at my very ears,
but rang and echoed and resounded as if
it were rolling and reverberated from the
vault of some cathedral, chanting in terrible
modulations. I heard the words quite
clearly.

"*Incipit liber iræ Domini Dei nostri.*

(Here beginneth The Book of the Wrath of the Lord our God.)

"And then the voice sang the word *Aleph*, prolonging it, it seemed through ages, and a light was extinguished as it began the chapter :

"*In that day, saith the Lord, there shall be a cloud over the land, and in the cloud a burning and a shape of fire, and out of the cloud shall issue forth my messengers ; they shall run all together, they shall not turn aside ; this shall be a day of exceeding bitterness, without salvation. And on every high hill, saith the Lord of Hosts, I will set my sentinels, and my armies shall encamp in the place of every valley ; in the house that is amongst rushes I will execute judgment, and in vain shall they fly for refuge to the munitions of the rocks. In the groves of the woods, in the places where the leaves are as a tent above them, they shall find the sword of the slayer ; and they that put their trust in walled cities shall be confounded. Woe unto the armed man, woe unto him that taketh pleasure in the strength of his artillery, for a little thing shall smite him, and by one that hath no might shall he be brought down into the dust. That which is low shall be set on*

*high ; I will make the lamb and the young
sheep to be as the lion from the swellings of
Jordan ; they shall not spare, saith the Lord,
and the doves shall be as the eagles on the
hill Engedi ; none shall be found that may
abide the onset of their battle.*

" Even now I can hear the voice rolling
far away, as if it came from the altar of a
great church and I stood at the door. There
are lights very far away in the hollow of a
vast darkness, and one by one they are
put out. I hear a voice chanting again
with that endless modulation that climbs
and aspires to the stars, and shines there,
and rushes down to the dark depths of
the earth, again to ascend ; the word
is *Zain*."

Here the manuscript lapsed again, and
finally into utter, lamentable confusion.
There were scrawled lines wavering across
the page on which Secretan seemed to have
been trying to note the unearthly music
that swelled in his dying ears. As the
scrapes and scratches of ink showed, he
had tried hard to begin a new sentence.
The pen had dropped at last out of his hand

upon the paper, leaving a blot and a smear
upon it.

Lewis heard the tramp of feet along the
passage ; they were carrying out the dead
to the cart.

## CHAPTER XIV

DR. LEWIS maintained that we should never begin to understand the real significance of life until we began to study just those aspects of it which we now dismiss and overlook as utterly inexplicable, and therefore, unimportant.

We were discussing a few months ago the awful shadow of the terror which at length had passed away from the land. I had formed my opinion, partly from observation, partly from certain facts which had been communicated to me, and the passwords having been exchanged, I found that Lewis had come by very different ways to the same end.

" And yet," he said, " it is not a true end, or rather, it is like all the ends of human inquiry, it leads one to a great mystery. We must confess that what has happened might have happened at any time in the history of the world. It did not happen till a year ago as a matter of fact, and therefore we made up our minds that it never could happen ; or, one would better say, it was outside the range even of imagination. But this is our way.

Most people are quite sure that the Black Death—otherwise the Plague—will never invade Europe again. They have made up their complacent minds that it was due to dirt and bad drainage. As a matter of fact the Plague had nothing to do with dirt or with drains; and there is nothing to prevent its ravaging England to-morrow. But if you tell people so, they won't believe you. They won't believe in anything that isn't there at the particular moment when you are talking to them. As with the Plague, so with the Terror. We could not believe that such a thing could ever happen. Remnant said, truly enough, that whatever it was, it was outside theory, outside our theory. Flatland cannot believe in the cube or the sphere."

I agreed with all this. I added that sometimes the world was incapable of seeing, much less believing, that which was before its own eyes.

"Look," I said, "at any eighteenth century print of a Gothic cathedral. You will find that the trained artistic eye even could not behold in any true sense the building that was before it. I have seen an old print of Peterborough Cathedral that looks as if the artist had drawn it from a clumsy model, constructed of bent wire and childrens' bricks."

"Exactly; because Gothic was outside the æsthetic theory (and therefore vision) of the time. You can't believe what you don't see: rather, you can't see what you don't believe. It was so during the time of the Terror. All this bears out what Coleridge said as to the necessity of having the idea before the facts could be of any service to one. Of course, he was right; mere facts, without the correlating idea, are nothing and lead to no conclusion. We had plenty of facts, but we could make nothing of them. I went home at the tail of that dreadful procession from Treff Loyne in a state of mind very near to madness. I heard one of the soldiers saying to the other: 'There's no rat that'll spike a man to the heart, Bill.' I don't know why, but I felt that if I heard any more of such talk as that I should go crazy; it seemed to me that the anchors of reason were parting. I left the party and took the short cut across the fields into Porth. I looked up Davies in the High Street and arranged with him that he should take on any cases I might have that evening, and then I went home and gave my man his instructions to send people on. And then I shut myself up to think it all out—if I could.

" You must not suppose that my experiences of that afternoon had afforded me the slightest illumination. Indeed, if it had not been that I had seen poor old Griffith's body lying pierced in his own farmyard, I think I should have been inclined to accept one of Secretan's hints, and to believe that the whole family had fallen a victim to a collective delusion or hallucination, and had shut themselves up and died of thirst through sheer madness. I think there have been such cases. It's the insanity of inhibition, the belief that you can't do something which you are really perfectly capable of doing. But ; I had seen the body of the murdered man and the wound that had killed him.

" Did the manuscript left by Secretan give me no hint ? Well, it seemed to me to make confusion worse confounded. You have seen it ; you know that in certain places it is evidently mere delirium, the wanderings of a dying mind. How was I

to separate the facts from the phantasms
—lacking the key to the whole enigma.
Delirium is often a sort of cloud-castle, a
sort of magnified and distorted shadow of
actualities, but it is a very difficult thing,
almost an impossible thing, to reconstruct
the real house from the distortion of it,
thrown on the clouds of the patient's
brain. You see, Secretan in writing that
extraordinary document almost insisted
on the fact that he was not in his proper
senses; that for days he had been part
asleep, part awake, part delirious. How
was one to judge his statement, to separate
delirium from fact? In one thing he
stood confirmed ; you remember he speaks
of calling for help up the old chimney of
Treff Loyne ; that did seem to fit in with
the tales of a hollow, moaning cry that had
been heard upon the Allt : so far one could
take him as a recorder of actual experiences.
And I looked in the old cellars of the farm
and found a frantic sort of rabbit-hole dug
by one of the pillars ; again he was confirmed. But what was one to make of that
story of the chanting voice, and the letters
of the Hebrew alphabet, and the chapter
out of some unknown Minor Prophet ?

When one has the key it is easy enough to sort out the facts, or the hints of facts from the delusions ; but I hadn't the key on that September evening.  I was forgetting the 'tree' with lights and fires in it ; that, I think, impressed me more than anything with the feeling that Secretan's story was, in the main, a true story.  I had seen a like appearance down there in my own garden ; but what was it ?

" Now, I was saying that, paradoxically, it is only by the inexplicable things that life can be explained.  We are apt to say, you know, ' a very odd coincidence ' and pass the matter by, as if there were no more to be said, or as if that were the end of it. Well, I believe that the only real path lies through the blind alleys."

" How do you mean ? "

" Well, this is an instance of what I mean.  I told you about Merritt, my brother-in-law, and the capsizing of that boat, the *Mary Ann*.  He had seen, he said, signal lights flashing from one of the farms on the coast, and he was quite certain that the two things were intimately connected as cause and effect.  I thought it all nonsense, and I was wondering how I

was going to shut him up when a big moth
flew into the room through that window,
fluttered about, and succeeded in burning
itself alive in the lamp.   That gave me my
cue ;   I asked Merritt if he knew why
moths made for lamps or something of the
kind ;   I thought it would be a hint to him
that I was sick of his flashlights and his
half-baked theories.   So it was—he looked
sulky and held his tongue.

" But a few minutes later I was called
out by a man who had found his little boy
dead in a field near his cottage about an
hour before.   The child was so still, they
said, that a great moth had settled on his
forehead and only fluttered away when they
lifted up the body.   It was absolutely
illogical ;  but it was this odd ' coincidence '
of the moth in my lamp and the moth on the
dead boy's forehead that first set me on the
track.   I can't say that it guided me in any
real sense ;  it was more like a great flare
of red paint on a wall ;  it rang up my
attention, if I may say so ;  it was a sort
of shock like a bang on the big drum.
No doubt Merritt was talking great nonsense that evening so far as his particular
instance went ;  the flashes of light from the

farm had nothing to do with the wreck of the boat. But his general principle was sound ; when you hear a gun go off and see a man fall it is idle to talk of ' a mere coincidence.' I think a very interesting book might be written on this question: I would call it ' A Grammar of Coincidence.'

" But as you will remember, from having read my notes on the matter, I was called in about ten days later to see a man named Cradock, who had been found in a field near his farm quite dead. This also was at night. His wife found him, and there were some very queer things in her story. She said that the hedge of the field looked as if it were changed ; she began to be afraid that she had lost her way and got into the wrong field. Then she said the hedge was lighted up as if there were a lot of glow-worms in it, and when she peered over the stile there seemed to be some kind of glimmering upon the ground, and then the glimmering melted away, and she found her husband's body near where this light had been. Now this man Cradock had been suffocated just as the little boy Roberts had been suffocated, and as that man in the Midlands who took a short cut one night had been

suffocated. Then I remembered that poor
Johnnie Roberts had called out about
'something shiny' over the stile just
before he played truant. Then, on my
part, I had to contribute the very remark-
able sight I witnessed here, as I looked
down over the garden ; the appearance
as of a spreading tree where I knew there
was no such tree, and then the shining and
burning of lights and moving colours.
Like the poor child and Mrs. Cradock, I had
seen something shiny, just as some man
in Stratfordshire had seen a dark cloud with
points of fire in it floating over the trees.
And Mrs. Cradock thought that the shape
of the trees in the hedge had changed.

" My mind almost uttered the word that
was wanted ; but you see the difficulties.
This set of circumstances could not, so far
as I could see, have any relation with the
other circumstances of the Terror. How
could I connect all this with the bombs and
machine-guns of the Midlands, with the
armed men who kept watch about the
munition shops by day and night ? Then
there was the long list of people here who
had fallen over the cliffs or into the quarry ;
there were the cases of the men stifled in

the slime of the marshes ; there was the affair of the family murdered in front of their cottage on the Highway ; there was the capsized *Mary Ann*. I could not see any thread that could bring all these incidents together ; they seemed to me to be hopelessly disconnected. I could not make out any relation between the agency that beat out the brains of the Williams's and the agency that overturned the boat. I don't know, but I think it's very likely if nothing more had happened that I should have put the whole thing down as an unaccountable series of crimes and accidents which chanced to occur in Meirion in the summer of 1915. Well, of course, that would have been an impossible standpoint in view of certain incidents in Merritt's story. Still, if one is confronted by the insoluble, one lets it go at last. If the mystery is inexplicable, one pretends that there isn't any mystery. That is the justification for what is called free thinking.

" Then came that extraordinary business of Treff Loyne. I couldn't put that on one side. I couldn't pretend that nothing strange or out of the way had happened. There was no getting over it or getting round it. I had seen with my eyes that there was a mystery, and a most horrible mystery. I have forgotten my logic, but one might say that Treff Loyne demonstrated the existence of a mystery in the figure of Death.

" I took it all home, as I have told you, and sat down for the evening before it. It appalled me, not only by its horror, but here again by the discrepancy between its terms. Old Griffith, so far as I could judge, had been killed by the thrust of a pike or perhaps of a sharpened stake : how could one relate this to the burning tree that had floated over the ridge of the barn. It was as if I said to you : ' here is a man drowned, and here is a man burned alive : show that each death was caused by the same agency ! ' And the moment that I left this particular case of Treff Loyne, and tried to get some light on it from other instances of the Terror, I would think of the man in the midlands who heard the feet of a thousand men rustling in the wood, and their voices as if dead men sat up in their bones and talked. And then I would say to myself, ' and how about that boat overturned in a calm sea ? '

There seemed no end to it, no hope of any solution.

"It was, I believe, a sudden leap of the mind that liberated me from the tangle. It was quite beyond logic. I went back to that evening when Merritt was boring me with his flashlights, to the moth in the candle, and to the moth on the forehead of poor Johnnie Roberts. There was no sense in it; but I suddenly determined that the child and Joseph Cradock the farmer, and that unnamed Stratfordshire man, all found at night, all asphyxiated, had been choked by vast swarms of moths. I don't pretend even now that this is demonstrated, but I'm sure it's true.

"Now suppose you encounter a swarm of these creatures in the dark. Suppose the smaller ones fly up your nostrils. You will gasp for breath and open your mouth. Then, suppose some hundreds of them fly into your mouth, into your gullet, into your windpipe, what will happen to you? You will be dead in a very short time, choked, asphyxiated."

"But the moths would be dead too. They would be found in the bodies."

"The moths? Do you know that it is

extremely difficult to kill a moth with cyanide of potassium ? Take a frog, kill it, open its stomach. There you will find its dinner of moths and small beetles, and the ' dinner ' will shake itself and walk off cheerily, to resume an entirely active existence. No ; that is no difficulty.

"Well, now I came to this. I was shutting out all the other cases. I was confining myself to those that came under the one formula. I got to the assumption, or conclusion, whichever you like, that certain people had been asphyxiated by the action of moths. I had accounted for that extraordinary appearance of burning or coloured lights that I had witnessed myself, when I saw the growth of that strange tree in my garden. That was clearly the cloud with points of fire in it that the Stratfordshire man took for a new and terrible kind of poison gas, that was the shiny something that poor little Johnnie Roberts had seen over the stile, that was the glimmering light that had led Mrs. Cradock to her husband's dead body, that was the assemblage of terrible eyes that had watched over Treff Loyne by night. Once on the right track I understood all this, for coming into this room in the dark, I have been amazed by the wonderful burning and the strange fiery colours of the eyes of a single moth, as it crept up the pane of glass, outside. Imagine the effect of myriads of such eyes, of the movement of these lights and fires in a vast swarm of moths, each insect being in constant motion while it kept its place in the mass : I felt that all this was clear and certain.

" Then the next step. Of course, we know nothing really about moths ; rather, we know nothing of moth reality. For all I know there may be hundreds of books which treat of moth and nothing but moth. But these are scientific books, and science only deals with surfaces ; it has nothing to do with realities—it is impertinent if it attempts to do with realities. To take a very minor matter ; we don't even know why the moth desires the flame. But we do know what the moth does not do ; it does not gather itself into swarms with the object of destroying human life. But here, by the hypothesis, were cases in which the moth had done this very thing ; the moth race had entered, it seemed, into a malignant conspiracy against the human race. It was

quite impossible, no doubt—that is to say,
it had never happened before—but I could
see no escape from this conclusion.

" These insects, then, were definitely
hostile to man ; and then I stopped, for I
could not see the next step, obvious though
it seems to me now. I believe that the
soldiers' scraps of talk on the way to
Treff Loyne and back flung the next plank
over the gulf. They had spoken of ' rat
poison,' of no rat being able to spike a man
through the heart ; and then, suddenly, I
saw my way clear. If the moths were
infected with hatred of men, and possessed
the design and the power of combining
against him ; why not suppose this hatred,
this design, this power shared by other non-
human creatures.

" The secret of the Terror might be
condensed into a sentence : the animals had
revolted against men.

" Now, the puzzle became easy enough ;
one had only to classify. Take the cases
of the people who met their deaths by falling
over cliffs or over the edge of quarries.
We think of sheep as timid creatures, who
always ran away. But suppose sheep that
don't run away ; and, after all, in reason

why should they run away? Quarry or
no quarry, cliff or no cliff; what would
happen to you if a hundred sheep ran after
you instead of running from you? There
would be no help for it; they would have
you down and beat you to death or stifle
you. Then suppose man, woman, or child
near a cliff's edge or a quarry-side, and a
sudden rush of sheep. Clearly there is no
help; there is nothing for it but to go
over. There can be no doubt that that is
what happened in all these cases.

"And again; you know the country and
you know how a herd of cattle will sometimes pursue people through the fields in a
solemn, stolid sort of way. They behave
as if they wanted to close in on you.
Townspeople sometimes get frightened and
scream and run; you or I would take no
notice, or at the utmost, wave our sticks
at the herd, which will stop dead or lumber
off. But suppose they don't lumber off.
The mildest old cow, remember, is stronger
than any man. What can one man or
half a dozen men do against half a hundred
of these beasts no longer restrained by that
mysterious inhibition, which has made for
ages the strong the humble slaves of the

weak ?   But if you are botanizing in the
marsh, like that poor fellow who was staying
at Porth, and forty or fifty young cattle
gradually close round you, and refuse to
move when you shout and wave your
stick, but get closer and closer instead, and
get you into the slime.  Again, where is
your help ?  If you haven't got an auto-
matic pistol, you must go down and stay
down, while the beasts lie quietly on you
for five minutes.  It was a quicker death
for poor Griffith of Treff Loyne—one of his
own beasts gored him to death with one
sharp thrust of its horn into his heart.
And from that morning those within the
house were closely besieged by their own
cattle and horses and sheep ; and when
those unhappy people within opened a
window to call for help or to catch a few
drops of rain water to relieve their burning
thirst, the cloud waited for them with its
myriad eyes of fire.  Can you wonder that
Secretan's statement reads in places like
mania ?  You perceive the horrible position of those people in Treff Loyne ; not
only did they see death advancing on them,
but advancing with incredible steps, as if
one were to die not only in nightmare but

by nightmare. But no one in his wildest,
most fiery dreams had ever imagined such
a fate. I am not astonished that Secretan
at one moment suspected the evidence of
his own senses, at another surmised that
the world's end had come."

" And how about the Williams's who
were murdered on the Highway near here ? "

" The horses were the murderers ; the
horses that afterwards stampeded the camp
below. By some means which is still
obscure to me they lured that family
into the road and beat their brains out ;
their shod hoofs were the instruments of
execution. And, as for the *Mary Ann*,
the boat that was capsized, I have no doubt
that it was overturned by a sudden rush of
the porpoises that were gambolling about
in the water of Larnac Bay. A porpoise
is a heavy beast—half a dozen of them could
easily upset a light rowing-boat. The
munition works ? Their enemy was rats.
I believe that it has been calculated that in
' greater London ' the number of rats is
about equal to the number of human
beings, that is, there are about seven
million of them. The proportion would be
about the same in all the great centres of

population; and the rat, moreover, is, on occasion, migratory in its habits. You can understand now that story of the *Semiramis*, beating about the mouth of the Thames, and at last cast away by Arcachon, her only crew dry heaps of bones. The rat is an expert boarder of ships. And so one can understand the tale told by the frightened man who took the path by the wood that led up from the new munition works. He thought he heard a thousand men treading softly through the wood and chattering to one another in some horrible tongue; what he did hear was the marshalling of an army of rats—their array before the battle.

"And conceive the terror of such an attack. Even one rat in a fury is said to be an ugly customer to meet; conceive then, the irruption of these terrible, swarming myriads, rushing upon the helpless, unprepared, astonished workers in the munition shops."

There can be no doubt, I think, that Dr. Lewis was entirely justified in these extraordinary conclusions. As I say, I had arrived at pretty much the same end,

by different ways ; but this rather as to the
general situation, while Lewis had made
his own particular study of those circumstances of the Terror that were within his
immediate purview, as a physician in
large practice in the southern part of
Meirion. Of some of the cases which he
reviewed he had, no doubt, no immediate
or first-hand knowledge ; but he judged
these instances by their similarity to the
facts which had come under his personal
notice. He spoke of the affairs of the
quarry at Llanfihangel on the analogy of
the people who were found dead at the
bottom of the cliffs near Porth, and he was
no doubt justified in doing so. He told
me that, thinking the whole matter over,
he was hardly more astonished by the
Terror in itself than by the strange way in
which he had arrived at his conclusions.

" You know," he said, " those certain
evidences of animal malevolence which
we knew of, the bees that stung the child
to death, the trusted sheepdog's turning
savage, and so forth. Well, I got no light
whatever from all this ; it suggested nothing
to me—simply because I had not got that
' idea ' which Coleridge rightly holds neces-

sary in all inquiry ; facts *qua* facts, as we said, mean nothing and, come to nothing. You do not believe, therefore you cannot see.

" And then, when the truth at last appeared it was through the whimsical ' coincidence,' as we call such signs, of the moth in my lamp and the moth on the dead child's forehead. This, I think, is very extraordinary."

" And there seems to have been one beast that remained faithful ; the dog at Treff Loyne. That is strange."

" That remains a mystery."

It would not be wise, even now, to describe too closely the terrible scenes that were to be seen in the munition areas of the north and the midlands during the black months of the Terror. Out of the factories issued at black midnight the shrouded dead in their coffins, and their very kinsfolk did not know how they had come by their deaths. All the towns were full of houses of mourning, were full of dark and terrible rumours ; incredible, as the incredible reality. There were things done and suffered that perhaps never will be

brought to light, memories and secret
traditions of these things will be whispered
in families, delivered from father to son,
growing wilder with the passage of the years,
but never growing wilder than the truth.

It is enough to say that the cause of the
Allies was for awhile in deadly peril. The
men at the front called in their extremity
for guns and shells. No one told them
what was happening in the places where
these munitions were made.

At first the position was nothing less
than desperate ; men in high places were
almost ready to cry "mercy" to the
enemy. But, after the first panic, measures
were taken such as those described by
Merritt in his account of the matter. The
workers were armed with special weapons,
guards were mounted, machine-guns were
placed in position, bombs and liquid flame
were ready against the obscene hordes of
the enemy, and the "burning clouds"
found a fire fiercer than their own. Many
deaths occurred amongst the airmen ; but
they, too, were given special guns, arms
that scattered shot broadcast, and so
drove away the dark flights that threatened
the airplanes.

And, then, in the winter of 1915–16, the Terror ended suddenly as it had begun. Once more a sheep was a frightened beast that ran instinctively from a little child ; the cattle were again solemn, stupid creatures, void of harm ; the spirit and the convention of malignant design passed out of the hearts of all the animals. The chains that they had cast off for awhile were thrown again about them.

And, finally, there comes the inevitable " why ? " Why did the beasts who had been humbly and patiently subject to man, or affrighted by his presence, suddenly know their strength and learn how to league together, and declare bitter war against their ancient master ?

It is a most difficult and obscure question. I give what explanation I have to give with very great diffidence, and an eminent disposition to be corrected, if a clearer light can be found.

Some friends of mine, for whose judgment I have very great respect, are inclined to think that there was a certain contagion of hate. They hold that the fury of the whole world at war, the great passion of death that seems driving all humanity to destruction, infected at last these lower creatures, and in place of their native instinct of submission, gave them rage and wrath and ravening.

This may be the explanation. I cannot say that it is not so, because I do not profess to understand the working of the universe. But I confess that the theory strikes me as fanciful. There may be a contagion of hate as there is a contagion of smallpox ; I do not know, but I hardly believe it.

In my opinion, and it is only an opinion, the source of the great revolt of the beasts is to be sought in a much subtler region of inquiry. I believe that the subjects revolted because the king abdicated. Man has dominated the beasts throughout the ages, the spiritual has reigned over the rational through the peculiar quality and grace of spirituality that men possess, that makes a man to be that which he is. And when he maintained this power and grace, I think it is pretty clear that between him and the animals there was a certain treaty and alliance. There was supremacy on the one hand, and submission on the other ; but at the same time there was between the two that cordiality which exists between lords and subjects in a well-organized state. I know a socialist who maintains that Chaucer's " Canterbury Tales " give a picture of true democracy. I do not know about that, but I see that knight and miller were able to get on quite pleasantly together, just because the knight knew that he was a knight and the miller knew that he was a miller. If the knight had had conscientious objections to his knightly grade, while the miller saw no reason why he should not be a knight, I am sure that their intercourse would have been difficult, unpleasant, and perhaps murderous.

So with man. I believe in the strength and truth of tradition. A learned man said to me a few weeks ago : " When I have to choose between the evidence of tradition and the evidence of a document. I always believe the evidence of tradition. Documents may be falsified, and often are falsified ; tradition is never falsified." This is true ; and, therefore, I think, one may put trust in the vast body of folklore which asserts that there was once a worthy and friendly alliance between man and the beasts.  Our popular tale of Dick Whittington and his Cat no doubt represents the adaptation of a very ancient legend to a comparatively modern personage, but we may go back into the ages and find the popular tradition asserting that not only are the animals the subjects, but also the friends of man.

All that was in virtue of that singular spiritual element in man which the rational animals do not possess.  Spiritual does not mean respectable, it does not even mean moral, it does not mean " good " in the ordinary acceptation of the word.  It signifies the royal prerogative of man, differencing him from the beasts.

For long ages he has been putting off this royal robe, he has been wiping the balm of consecration from his own breast.  He has declared, again and again, that he is not spiritual, but rational, that is, the equal of the beasts over whom he was once sovereign.  He has vowed that he is not Orpheus but Caliban.

But the beasts also have within them something which corresponds to the spiritual quality in men—we are content to call it instinct.  They perceived that the throne was vacant—not even friendship was possible between them and the self-deposed monarch. If he were not king he was a sham, an impostor, a thing to be destroyed.

Hence, I think, the Terror. They have risen once—they may rise again.

PRINTED AT THE COMPLETE PRESS
WEST NORWOOD
LONDON S.E.